Hurl the demons back to hell

K.O. was staring across the river at the low green mound of an island. "That's got to be it, you think?"

"Gotta be," replied Rafael.

"Be cool then. The jungle blots up sound. There could be—"

Suddenly K.O. gripped Rafael's arm and pointed with his 9mm Luger. They saw sunlight glinting off helmets. Uniformed killers in rowboats were emerging from behind the island.

"Damn, damn, damn," said Rafael. "A whole new ball game."

In seconds, Phoenix Force would have to blast those targets into the air, would pin them for an instant with another burst, then let them drop— bundles of bloody rags.

Pure survival instinct, to grant butchery its bloody reward. Power to you, Phoenix!

PHOENIX FORCE

#1 Argentine Deadline
#2 Guerilla Games

PHOENIX FORCE

AN EXECUTIONER SERIES

Guerilla Games

Don Pendleton & Gar Wilson

A GOLD EAGLE BOOK FROM

WORLDWIDE

TORONTO · NEW YORK · LOS ANGELES · LONDON

First edition June 1982

ISBN 0-373-61302-4

Special thanks and acknowledgment to Dan Marlowe
for his contributions to this work.

Printed in Canada

As the world becomes smaller, it becomes
more violent. Foreign soil is dangerous.
This book is dedicated to all those
who serve their country overseas.

Phoenix Force is Mack Bolan's latest weapon: five extraordinary men, forged in the final flames of Mack's anti-Mafia campaign to rise as the world's leading anti-terrorist team.

Katz—a French-Israeli intelligence veteran with one arm. Unbeatable in combat.

Gary Manning—a Canadian explosives engineer. Incredibly strong, he thrives on trouble.

Keio Ohara—a Japanese master of martial arts. Unusually tall. Unusually deadly.

David McCarter—a British brawler, famous for his SAS activities. Rude. Rugged. Ruthless.

Rafael Encizo—a survivor of Castro's prisons, expert in underwater warfare. Altogether fearless.

1

Ian Revill unfastened his seat belt when the dark green forest below leveled out beneath the plane. "I'll nip back for a spot of babysitting, Charlie," he said to the pilot.

Charles Gargan nodded. He was a thin-faced man with a drooping reddish gray mustache and almost white muttonchop whiskers. Both men wore khaki bush uniforms, semi-military in cut but with no insignia. "They look as if they could use it," Gargan said. "I can't recall the last time I saw such a set of frozen-faced human beings."

Revill threw back the locking arm on the cockpit door and stepped back into the cabin. The man called Willoughby, the only one to whom he'd been introduced, was on his feet. Sixtyish, Revill thought. And exhausted looking. The other five passengers, three men and two women, sat three or four seats apart on both sides of the aisle, with no two people seated close together. The cabin configuration provided for a maximum of twenty-six passengers.

Revill waited while Willoughby went from occupied seat to occupied seat, speaking a word or two to each individual and giving each nearer shoulder a squeeze before returning to his own seat at the rear of the plane. Revill walked down the aisle and took the seat across from him.

"I'm the second officer, Mr. Willoughby," he began. "Ian Revill. Our captain is Charles Gargan. I'm sorry neither of us had the opportunity for a chat before takeoff, but right then takeoff seemed to take priority."

"Ray Willoughby," the other man said. "Certainly none of us would quarrel with that." His attempt at a smile was tired looking, and his voice was almost a whisper. He also spoke with a slight stammer. "The Bolivian guerillas are not pleasant people."

"You were held how long?" Revill asked.

"Ninety-four days. Not the longest time, not the shortest." Willoughby tried again to smile. "Just an eternity."

"There seems to be a certain amount of apathy among your colleagues," Revill said. "Are there any injuries or other things I should be aware of?"

"Well, I guess you should know a little about each of us," Willoughby sighed. "We're all in pretty much the same shape. Exhausted, and psychologically traumatized. The ladies had it especially rough. Muriel Miller, the attractive blonde, was continually abused. She's our PR lady. From New York. Jennifer Gossage, the brunette, she just had her fiftieth birthday. She's our financial VP, from Washington. She's lost forty pounds, and was thin to begin with. She's totally withdrawn into herself. A basket case."

"Terry Conrad there, the young man reading the magazine, seems to be holding on. He's from New Jersey. He does all our photography. This is one assignment he won't forget. They took all his equipment and film the first day."

"Harold Dobbins, asleep beneath the blanket, is our economics expert. He's fairly new to ISL. Very quiet. But very bright. And tough. He's paid for it, too. He has been brutally beaten and starved. A good man."

"What about him," Revill asked, "the husky gent with the beard?"

"That's Holt. Kenneth J. Holt. Of the Boston Holts. A senior VP and considered one of the potential successors to the presidency of Intercontinental. We don't get along. I guess he thinks he should be the senior man on this junket. Maybe so. Anyway, he's held up well. A tough customer, but smart enough to avoid trouble. Was a real ladies' man until this little vacation got under way. Now he keeps to himself and continually writes. I don't know what. He keeps it all to himself. Strange behavior, for a Holt."

Willoughby laughed. "We are a motley crew. Certainly don't look like we did when we left Kennedy in New York. And we really haven't seen all that much of each other during our capture. Except for—ahh—group, er, displays. The obscene games those guerillas played with us. We're still attempting to emerge into the real world. Say, I assume Intercontinental ransomed us after all, eh?"

"Yes," Revill said. "And they chartered this plane to fly you out to Bolivia. I expected we'd take you to Rio, but our flight plan says Buenos Aires."

"Intercontinental has a branch in Buenos Aires," Willoughby explained. "I'd rather doubted we'd be ransomed at all at this late date, you know. Bad precedent and all that. It made it hard to attempt to keep up morale. Do you happen to know how much money we were worth to Intercontinental?" His attempt at a smile was even thinner looking than before. One of the women stood up beside her seat and looked back at Willoughy. "Be with you in a minute, Muriel," he called.

"I've heard a figure of six and a half million mentioned," Revill said carefully. "Dollars. But that's only gossip. You feel your group's abduction was political?"

"At first I thought it was solely for the money, and I'm sure that was important to them, too. But the negotiations went on for so long I came to believe there was something of a political nature also in all the pulling and hauling. The guerillas seemed determined to make their mark upon us capitalists for all the world to observe before our departure." He moved away from what was obviously a painful subject. "What sort of plane is this? I've done a lot of flying, and I saw the two turboprop engines when we came aboard, but I don't believe I've seen an aircraft exactly like it before."

Revill laughed. "I doubt you have. There weren't many of them built in the first place, and there aren't many still operative except in backwaters of the world. The plane is a Nord-62, often called a Nord Broussard. It was built in France in the 60s by Nord Aviation, a company that was taken over in the 70s by Aerospatiale."

"We don't seem to be flying very high," Willoughby observed.

"The flight charts say we should encounter nothing above 3800 feet in this part of the world," Revill said. "Although charts for the southern half of the Southern Hemisphere are never totally reliable." He slapped the seat beside him. "But she's a tough old girl, well-suited to the country. We have a cruising speed of 250 mph, although we rarely push it much above 225, and a range of 650 miles."

Willoughby had been listening in the manner of a man absorbed by inner thought. At the last statement, he turned his head to look directly at Revill. "Then we'll need to refuel before we reach Beunos Aires."

"That's right. But we've map-plotted the trip—" Revill leaned out across the aisle toward Willoughby "—so that our first brief stop will be in Bahia Negra, which is across the Paraguayan border. We have clearance from the Paraguayan government to over-fly their territory en route to Buenos Aires. With that bit of cooperation on our plate, it seemed foolish to even consider landing inside Bolivian borders again."

"I quite agree," Willoughby said. "Where did you pick us up? We had no idea where we were after they moved us out of La Paz."

"You were brought out of the forest in a truck and—ahh—dumped on the airport runway at a town called Potrero. It's a fair-sized place, but isolated." Revill rose from his seat. "I'll get back to the cockpit and spell Captain Gargan. If there's anything you feel we can do for you, I hope you'll let us know."

"Do you get many errands of mercy like this?" Willoughby asked.

Revill smiled. "Charter pilots are never surprised at whatever the luck of the draw brings up. We're pleased to be able to be of some assistance to you."

He walked back down the aisle, noting in passing

the untouched wrapped sandwiches and bottles of soft drinks he and Charles had brought aboard. "Zombies," he said to Gargan when he sat down in the copilot's seat again.

"Sheep," Gargan corrected him. "They've been wrung out. God knows what happened to them in the hands of that lot of *mestizos* we saw at Potrero." He looked at his watch. "We'll have them out of Bolivian territory in an hour and a half, and after that it'll be a piece of cake."

The flight continued in silence.

"Bahia Negra coming up," Gargan announced after what seemed to Revill a long time. Gargan circled a narrow runway, looking for a wind sock. "I swear they hide the things on purpose. Creates a little excitement for them, I suppose. Ahh, there it is." He put the plane down skillfully and taxied to the fuel pumps.

He left the cockpit as a gray colored Jeep bounced out to meet them. Revill followed him and opened the cabin door, then dropped a three-step platform. A Paraguayan Air Force lieutenant came aboard and looked curiously at the passengers.

"Greetings," Revill said in Spanish.

"Thou, also," the officer returned.

"You have been informed there are no papers with this flight?"

"We know. Godspeed."

The lieutenant saluted and departed, and Revill went outside in the burning heat to supervise the refueling. The thirty-five minute task took almost ninety minutes.

With Revill at the controls, they got under way

again and headed almost directly south instead of the southeasterly course they had been flying previously above the Gran Chaco swamps. After an hour, Captain Gargan unbuckled his seat belt and rose from the copilot's seat.

"I'll check on our sheep," he said. "Perhaps they've livened up a bit. Although I don't know what—"

There was a whistling roar from above them and a shock wave struck the Nord. It vibrated sharply and the wings trembled. "What the hell was *that*?" Gargan exclaimed. He had half fallen back into his seat.

"Buzzed," Revill said tersely. He pointed toward the western sky. "No markings I could see." His voice rose. "Here he comes again!"

A large, swept-wing aircraft seemed headed directly at them for an instant. It curled off to one side while a double stream of machine-gun tracer bullets zipped down into the forest below. The plane disappeared from sight, moving at terrific speed, and the shock wave came up from beneath and again buffeted the Nord.

"North American Super Sabre!" Revill's voice was still raised.

"A fighter plane, Ian?"

"That's a Sabre," Revill declared positively. "It's still the principal fighter plane of twenty-five of the world's smaller air forces. But not Paraguay's." He had turned his head to see out the side cockpit window. "A nasty job of work, even though it's thirty-five years since it first flew. If— Look!"

Charles Gargan was already looking. The Sabre

had slid into view alongside them, on Revill's side. The Sabre pilot repeatedly and vigorously jerked a black-gloved thumb toward the ground.

"Look at the sonofabitch," Revill said angrily. "He can hardly throttle down to our speed. He's telling us to land."

Gargan reached for the radio microphone. "I'll try to raise Asunción."

"You did see those machine guns firing, Charlie?" There was an edge in Revill's voice. "What are our responsibilities to these passengers? And to ourselves?"

Gargan withdrew his hand. The Sabre pilot was sweeping his right arm in a wide arc. "He's ordering us to follow him," Revill interpreted.

"So follow," Gargan said curtly. "We haven't even a pistol aboard this perambulator." He tugged hard at one end of his mustache.

Revill showed a thumbs-up gesture of obedience, then waggled the Nord's wingtips in a universal signal of acknowledgment. Gargan was staring at the clipboard beside his seat. It contained a flight chart folded to their current position. "It's got to be Concepción where he intends us to land," he muttered.

"What does the chart show for the runway there?"

"Dirt," Gargan replied. "Four thousand feet." He bent closer to the chart. "That's estimated. Unverified."

"Means we can get in there but he can't, Charlie."

"Stop dreaming, Ian. When he forces us down, do you doubt there'll be a welcoming committee?"

"But we have clearance from the Paraguayan Air Force itself!"

"No markings, remember?" Gargan said. "This is a pirate plane. It could mean anything. And probably nothing good." He rose from his seat again. "I'll go back and try to say something soothing to our poor sheep."

He unlocked the cockpit door and entered the cabin. Babbling wildly, the previously lethargic passengers were clustered at the front windows.

"Ladies and gentlemen," Gargan began. "There has been a slight but temporary change of plan that requires—"

They turned upon him en masse.

"I knew it was too good to be true!" the woman called Muriel shrieked at him in a voice bordering on hysteria. She had blond hair with black roots showing through. "I knew it! I knew it!"

Gargan could feel the suddenly reduced power of the Nord's engines and the slight settling movement as Ian Revill prepared to land.

2

Rafael "Pescado" Encizo continued to punch into his desk calculator the figures he was adding while he reached for the ringing telephone in his small Miami office. *"Sí?"* he said. He had a squared-off face with heavy brows and a cleft chin.

"Stony Man here, Rafael," Mack Bolan's unmistakable voice said in Encizo's ear. "Call me back."

"You've got it, man," Rafael said in English. He was already surging to his feet at the same time he replaced the telephone receiver. Stocky, and with heavy upper-body musculature, he still moved with grace and deceptive speed.

He unlocked the center drawer in his desk and removed the portable phone scrambler designed and built by Keio Ohara, the Japanese giant known as KO, and an integral part of Phoenix Force.

Encizo shoved the leather case containing the scrambler under his jacket, pinning it between his arm and body. He left the office quickly after double-checking that he had locked the door behind him.

He ran down the single flight of stairs to the street. Call Bolan back, eh? He felt a rising tide of expectation. These oddball calls at oddball hours often led to oddball assignments. If this were one, it would be good to have Phoenix Force assembled again.

He passed by the first two pay phones on street corners in favor of one that was in a booth in a darkened rear corner of a drugstore. He removed the leather case from under his jacket while he stood with his back to the drugstore proper. Encizo carefully applied KO's device to the receiver's mouthpiece and secured it with its own snap-on clamp and mouthpiece extension. He had no idea how the thing worked. He had asked KO once, but the tall Japanese had just smiled and offered an electronic monologue Rafael couldn't follow.

He dialed the number he had no need to look up and waited for Mack Bolan's voice to reply. "Stony Man," Bolan said. His voice on the scrambler had a mechanically scratchy sound that required close attention.

"Pescado," Encizo said, using his nickname. His own voice had a hollow sound in his ear.

"We've got a nasty one," Bolan said. "In Bolivia. Or Paraguay."

"It would help to know which," Rafael said mildly. "Those two governments despise each other."

"If you put me to the wall, I'd say Paraguay," Bolan returned. "Perhaps you can judge after you hear the story, which is that three months ago, six U.S. civilians, four men and two women, all of whom worked for the same U.S. multinational corporation, were kidnapped by Bolivian leftist guerillas and held for ransom."

"So it's Bolivia?" Encizo interrupted.

"After lengthy negotiations," Bolan continued, "the corporation paid five and a half million for the release of their people, who were put aboard a chartered plane to be flown to Buenos Aires. The Paraguayan government okayed a flyover of their territory to keep the flight within the limitations of the charter aircraft.''

"Someone must really have twisted General Stroessner's arm to obtain that kind of guarantee,'' Encizo observed.

"Yeah, they are a powerful multinational. Anyway, when the plane was an hour inside Paraguayan territory, it went off the radar screens, including a couple of private ones.''

"Shot down," Rafael said softly. "But no, wait a moment. If the general had wanted to embarrass Bolivia, he'd have had the plane downed over Bolivian territory, not his own.''

"How about it being taken down by guerillas in Paraguay who wanted to embarrass Stroessner?''

"I like that better," Rafael said. "Except that I wouldn't care to be those guerillas if Stroessner can retaliate, because he won't take kindly to the violation of his safe passage agreement. There's another possibility, Mack. Paraguayan guerillas, with their nationalistic hatred for everthing Bolivian, might have decided to show the world they know how to squeeze a multinational in a proper manner.'' He paused for an instant. "Why should Stony Man or Phoenix Force be interested in all this?''

"The multinational doesn't know that one of its employees in the kidnapped group is also an important agency man.''

"Ahh, I see. And Phoenix is to go in and liberate him?''

"The preference is to liberate them all, but if that isn't possible, your answer is yes.''

Rafael's thoughts had been ranging ahead. "Isn't it possible the original Bolivian guerillas could have rekidnapped the group as a means to taking another bite out of the corporate bankroll? Although I guess it's likely they'd have complicated their operation by waiting until the plane was inside Paraguay's borders.

"There's a side bar to that," Bolan said. "The corporation actually considered the possible loss of the kidnapped group. They didn't want to set themselves up for similar smash-and-grab operations around the world. They were pressured, negotiated and, eventually, paid off. Now they've got nothing to show for it."

"You're saying they won't help again?"

"What would you do if you were chairman of the board of Intercontinental Systems Ltd., and had to explain such deficit financing to stockholders in twelve countries? I'd say they definitely won't move quickly. As usual, Rafael, we don't have much time. The others are on their way to Miami to join you, and you will all meet in your office at 5:00 P.M. tomorrow. A messenger will hand-deliver to you, tomorrow morning, all the paperwork I presently have on this. So far it isn't much. Right now I don't even have the cover name of the CIA agent. Come to think of it, I don't know if it's a man or a woman."

"Either way," Rafael said. "Whatever it takes."

"It's another get-in-and-get-out job," Bolan said. "Improvisation will count for a great deal more than long-range planning. Call me before the group leaves Miami, Rafael, in case I have any last-minute information. And keep the shiny side up and the rubber side down."

The mechanical scratchiness in Encizo's ear ceased.

He uncoupled the scrambler, put it back into its case, shoved the case under his jacket, and left the drugstore.

He smiled all the way back to his office.

The first thing he did after unlocking the door was to look at his desk calendar. His smile disappeared. He had made a date with Antoinette for tomorrow night. He sat down rubbing his chin. Finally he shrugged and reached for his telephone. "Something has come up, *querida*—"

"You're not breaking our date again, Rafael!"

"What can I do? It's business."

"I don't believe it's business! I think you've found a young girl!"

"Querida," he said soothingly, "you know I've always felt that the older the violin, the sweeter the music."

"Are you saying I'm *old*?"

"Of course not! Of course not! I'm saying merely that I appreciate the fruit of maturity."

"What a silver-tongued gigolo you are, Rafael! For how long shall I expect you to be absent this time?"

"Not long, Toni. Not long. I swear it. And then— is your telephone receiver heating up in your hand?"

"Imbecile!" she snorted, and hung up on him.

Rafael smiled, hung up the phone, and began making a list of the salient points of his conversation with Mack Bolan.

3

Ian Revill was the last person off the plane. He had remained in the pilot's seat of the Nord at the end of the bumpy, dusty runway, shutting down switches and running through his post-flight checklist. It was the only thing to do if they ever expected the Nord to fly them out of there.

When he emerged into scorching sunlight, there were about twenty armed men around the aircraft, all of them obviously jubilant at forcing down "the big bird" he heard them referring to in Guarani-Spanish, the mixed Indian-Spanish mode of Paraguayan expression. The six passengers and crew were lined up against the side of the Nord, confronted by Indian-looking men wearing dark green, tattered, sweat-stained uniforms, narrow-brimmed black hats, and criss-crossed bandoliers.

Three men with carbines guarded the group while the rest of the guerillas eagerly explored the inside of the plane. One by one they emerged, grinning, each carrying an item of booty, generally worthless, consisting of anything loose they found inside. Revill watched apprehensively as Charles Gargan, standing beside him, glowered at the invaders.

Gargan started to say something, and Revill nudged him. When Gargan turned impatiently in his direction, Revill shook his head in a slow negative. After an instant Gargan nodded, but he continued to view the despoliation with compressed lips.

There was no mistaking the guerilla who was in charge. He was a short, chunky man with a dirty-looking beard and huge eyes. He was the only one among the men who was hatless, disclosing a shock of bushy black hair. Revill heard the men call him Chama, which he understood to mean "man of fire."

Chama had a blustering voice and an air of self-importance. He was the only one of the guerillas with an automatic weapon. He had a submachine gun slung by its strap in reverse over his right shoulder, with the stubby barrel pointing toward the ground.

There had been no spectators at this landing. A truck, an ancient-looking six by six, emerged from the scrubby trees beyond. Most of the nearby forest appeared to consist of nearly impenetrable thick brush and waist-high weeds.

Chama demanded in passable Spanish that his prisoners board the truck. Revill noticed that the dangerous-looking guerilla leader also produced a few words of English. The group from the plane shuffled forward silently through the powdery dust and one by one hoisted themselves up into the rear of the truck. The men from Intercontinental offered no assistance to the women. Despite their ninety-plus days of forced comradeship, the members of the group didn't even appear to like each other. Revill wondered if perhaps it was only because of their captivity.

He saw Muriel, the younger woman who had

seemed close to hysterics while disembarking, say something to Ray Willoughby, who ignored her. Revill didn't dwell upon it, because he had a problem of his own. He was still watching Charles Gargan closely. Shut up, Charlie, Revill pleaded silently. Life to these people means nothing. This is no time to be filing a complaint with the commissioner.

The truck rolled down a slight grade to the river which Revill had seen from the Nord but which was a surprisingly short distance away. An unpainted, low-lying barge was sitting in a backwater, almost beached as it was so far removed from the river's current. Two ridiculously tiny outboard motors were attached to its stern.

A canted plank led from the river's edge to the deck of the barge. Two guerillas ran up it lightly, then beckoned to the prisoners. Revill watched while the thin plank, sagging in the middle of its length, dumped Harold and Jennifer on the muddy bank before they learned to go up it one at a time and avoid the plank's waves of movement created by someone else. The guerillas thought it was hilarious.

Once on deck, the prisoners were herded into a shallow cockpit area where, by stretching out flat in dirty bilge water, they were below gunwale level and out of sight. While boarding, Revill had seen a primitive rudder at the barge's stern.

Chama's men poled the barge out of the backwater while their leader started up the outboard engines. The barge crept out into the current, where to Revill's surprise, Chama headed upstream. They crawled along at a mile or two an hour through the muddy, menacing-looking water.

It took them almost an hour to edge their way past what Revill knew had to be the town of Concepción, off the port bow. North of town the river widened, and within another few hundred yards it broadened into a lake. All this time Chama said nothing to his captives. He just glared at them, singly, as if daring anyone to talk.

A small island appeared in the lake, then another. When a third, quite a bit larger, loomed up, Chama steered the barge in a long loop until they were beyond the island at its upper end. He cut his outboards then, letting the barge drift backward to the island. As they neared shore, Revill could see in the midst of shoreline greenery a gouged-out muddy area where landings had obviously been made many times before. Back from the shore he could see two dilapidated-looking, vine-covered huts.

The barge slid up onto the mud with a sucking sound, and guerillas poured over both sides into the shallow, brackish-looking water and then waded ashore. Shouts and arm waving indicated that the prisoners were to do likewise. Revill stood up, walked to the stern which overhung the beached part of the barge, and jumped down two and a half feet to dry ground. He could hear the guerillas jabbering among themselves about the strange creatures who went out of their way just to avoid a little river water and mud. So far Revill had heard nothing from the guerillas that would indicate any feeling of animosity. Yet, in Chama's face there was a definite expression of disdain. His near-bulging eyes often stared at Revill with what seemed a lunatic's leer.

The rest of the prisoners followed Revill's example

in disembarking. The two women were last off the barge except for Gargan. Next to last was the youngest-looking woman, Muriel. She half-crouched, hesitating, looking down with dismay at the slight drop.

Chama beckoned to her imperiously, and when she still hesitated, he moved closer to the barge's stern. Muriel closed her eyes and leaped off the barge. Grinning hugely, Chama jumped closer and intercepted her downward flight. Muriel landed with her crotch on the stocky guerilla's palm. Her weight forced his arm downward momentarily, but his strength was such that he raised her up again immediately until her toes were off the ground.

Muriel screamed loudly while Chama laughed uproariously. She clawed at his face, which he averted, still laughing. When he did look at her, she spat full in his face. The laughter stopped. Chama dumped Muriel to the ground. He took two quick steps backward, at the same time jerking his right shoulder with a practiced twitch until the submachine gun came into his hands. He aimed it at Muriel, still on the ground.

"Oh, I say, now!" Charles Gargan said from the stern of the barge.

"Charlie!" Ian Revill warned.

But Chama, in a rage, had already turned to confront Gargan. "You say w'at?" he shrieked. "W'at, airplane man?"

"I say you're an imbecile. An ignorant, pop-eyed beast!" Gargan screamed in accumulated, uncontrollable rage.

Revill thought despairingly that Chama undoubt-

edly understood Gargan's meaning, if not the defini-
tion. The submachine gun barrel was already swing-
ing around in line with Gargan's head. The Nord's
pilot never flinched. A short burst of no more than a
dozen bullets obliterated Gargan's head. The impact
was such that it knocked his body sideways from the
barge into the muddy slough where it remained motionless, with only the feet protruding out of the
muddy, slowly reddening water.

Ian Revill felt his own features tightening up, muscle by muscle, into a stolid, impassive mask.

Chama swung around toward his men, none of
whom looked surprised. Chama indicated Muriel.
"Take her inside and strap her down!" he bellowed
in Spanish.

4

David McCarter and Yakov Katzenelenbogen were the first to arrive at Rafael's Miami office for the Phoenix Force meeting. "I happened to be in London when I received Mack's call—" Yak explained during handshakes "—so David and I flew over together." Yak's handshake was left-handed, although he was wearing his right-arm prosthetic device that attached just below his elbow. He was a craggy-faced man with close-cropped hair textured like steel wool.

"Did Mack fill you in?" Rafael asked.

"Only to the point of having me contact colleagues and pinpoint the area of the problem."

"What's it really about this time?" McCarter demanded. He was typically British in appearance, light haired and fair skinned. His apparently easygoing disposition was belied by a suspicious nature and a blowtorch temper. His handshake disclosed his permanently bent little finger that was his souvenir of a grenade explosion in Laos.

"Let's wait for the others and save repetition," Rafael suggested. "Here's someone now."

He opened his office door after again peering out through the miniature peephole. Gary Manning strode into the office, barrel chested and thick thighed. His physical presence was such that he seemed to take up more space than his five-foot ten and 190-pound physique demanded. His ruddy, weathered features proclaimed the confirmed outdoor man.

"Where's KO?" he wanted to know after ebullient handshakes and back-slapping all around.

"Should be here any minute," Rafael replied. He drew chairs up to his desk—chairs borrowed from neighboring offices—then placed ashtrays in front of two of the chairs. "That's yours—" he said to Yak, pointing "—and the other is for KO when he gets here. And I'll ask the pair of you not to fog up the rest of us completely."

"We can't all be ascetics," Yak said comfortably, glancing down at his unfiltered Camel cigarette in the grip of his prosthetic right hand.

"Ascetics?" Manning gibed. "How's your love life, Rafael?"

"Intermittent," Rafael said with a smile. "But no complaints."

There was a loud knock upon the office door. Rafael went to it, looked out, and opened it again. Keio Ohara entered with a high-armed wave for all. Rafael reached out and snatched a thin, black cigar from the corner of KO's mouth, then bear hugged him in a chest-bruising embrace. They danced stiff leggedly from side to side for an instant in the manner of waltzing bears before Rafael stepped back and restored the cigar to his friend's mouth. Keio Ohara's features looked more Chinese than those of the Japanese national that he was. He had wide cheekbones, an improperly set broken nose that had resulted in a flat bridge, and a firm chin. He was the youngest of the group.

"Chairs, in your chairs everyone," Rafael ordered as group members paired off in quick greetings. "Let's get this show on the road."

The group seated itself amidst a prolonged shuffling of feet as the men tried to find almost nonexistent legroom around the small desk.

"To our mutton," Rafael said, picking up the notes he had made after his conversation with Mack Bolan. He read them to the group. "Yak has more for us," he concluded.

Katzenelenbogen nodded. "When Mack told me on the phone that the problem was probably centered in Paraguay, I called a few academic friends in Asunción to see what was on the breeze there. One knew about a so-called mercy flight under Paraguayan guarantees that had been forced down north of the capital. He thought it might be in the area of Concepción, a port on the Paraguay River."

"That's what we need—" Rafael began, then checked himself. "Yak? Why don't you chair the meeting?"

"You've been the point man to now," Yak refused. "You wield the whip and chair. You've had more time to think about it than the rest of us. And once we're on the ground there your polyglot Spanish will certainly be more serviceable than my textbook proficiency."

"Okay," Rafael agreed. He glanced around the table. "I started to say a second ago that what we needed to know is where these people are being held, with some degree of accuracy, because if we get bogged down in looking for them it could take longer than the rest of our combined lives."

Ostentatiously, he moved KO's ashtray a foot farther away from himself. KO smiled and moved it back. "I know a little bit about Paraguay," Rafael resumed, "and what I learned about it surprised me. It's a very, very, very primitive country. When you're talking about flying there, you're talking about flying into Asunción, period. That's it. Roads in the whole country total only twelve thousand kilometers, of which only one thousand are paved. When it rains, the unpaved roads are closed. There is one railroad line of four hundred kilometers that runs from Asunción to Encarnación on the Rio Paraná, the wrong direction for us if Concepción is actually our target point."

"Car rentals?" Manning suggested.

"Possibly. But there are only forty thousand vehicles in the country, two-thirds of them military and commercial. Any vehicle is worth a few times its weight in gold. And there are all those unpaved roads to contend with. No, we need to drop in on Asunción and find a quick fix to go north."

"What are we dealing with in the way of opposition?" McCarter asked.

"Terrorists," Rafael said bluntly. "No one else would dare to pull hairs from Stroessner's beard in his own bailiwick."

"What about weapons?" Manning inquired.

Rafael looked toward McCarter. "Do you still have a string on that French munitions-type in Rio, David?"

"Sweetie-Pie Sazerac?" McCarter smiled. "He still owes me a big one, if that's what you mean. He can be trusted. If *I'm* involved."

"That's what I mean. We've got to fly to Asunción

via Rio de Janeiro, anyway, so why don't you stop off and do a deal with the guy?'' He passed slips of paper around the table. "Anyone want to add anything to this list?'' He waited a moment while the lists were studied. No one spoke. "Okay, David, take Gary with you. KO—'' Rafael tossed his car keys across the desk so they landed in KO's ashtray and dumped into his lap "—shoot on out to the airport,'' he continued as if nothing had happened. "Pick up five tickets, two to Rio, three to Asunción, Varig flight nine hundred leaving at nine o'clock tonight.'' He turned to Yak. "That will get us into Asunción at a little after noon tomorrow.''

KO had already picked up the car keys. He rose, walked around behind Rafael while the latter was speaking to Yak, and wiped the ashes from the car keys off on the back of Rafael's shirt. "Hey!'' Rafael exclaimed.

KO grinned at him. "Whenever you dive, Pescado, make sure of the depth of the pool.'' He was still grinning when he went out the door.

Rafael was smiling, too. "David,'' he went on, "no time for haggling with your man Sweetie-Pie about prices. Of course he'll hit you up for double or triple top dollar.''

"So why should we play charity society for that little piranha?'' McCarter demanded.

"Because when you've struck the deal and put the cash in his hot little hand, *then* you tell him of course he's flying the goods into Paraguay for you. He'll squeal like a pig with its tail caught in a gate, but he won't let go of the money, either. He'll do it. And you and Gary will be on his plane with him to make sure he doesn't change his mind about which direction he's taking."

Gary started to laugh. "You Cubans are something else," he said. "Talk about devious."

"You've only heard half of it," Rafael grinned. "Once on the ground in Paraguay near Concepción, we co-opt Sweetie-Pie and his plane into the whole operation. He and his plane could be our ticket out of there if we're a little pushed."

Yak was nodding his head slowly. "It sounds good," he said. "It sounds tight. How do the three of us coming up from Asunción link up with David and Gary?"

"With these." Rafael went to the wall closet, unlocked it, and separated five walkie-talkies from two dozen in the closet. He passed them around. "I'll put KO's in my luggage. Anything else? No? Okay, let's meet in the International Lounge at the airport at seven thirty for dinner."

"Won't they feed us on the plane?" Manning asked.

"Sure, but since when did you ever object to eating twice?"

Gary's caloric intake was notorious. They all pushed back from the desk, stretching in relief.

"What's the tune to 'Paraguay, here we come'?" David inquired. "Give me the key and I'll whistle it."

"You just whistle 'Dixie' to the Frenchman and we won't have to worry about stopping the tide," Rafael retorted. "We'll move the goddamn beach."

The meeting broke up.

5

Ian Revill stood with the five prisoners while Muriel was carried inside the hut. Four guerillas picked her up by an arm or a leg each and carried her inside like a sack of cordwood. She had screamed once when first swung off the ground, but had then become silent.

They stood there in mind-scrambling heat, still menaced by carbine-wielding guerillas. Revill could feel perspiration trickling from his armpits down his sides, and from the back of his neck under his shirt collar down his back. He knew it wasn't only the stifling heat that contributed to his clamminess.

The group had a gut-churning, five-minute wait before the carbines motioned them inside the hut. It was so dark inside after the blazing sunlight outside that Revill had to wait for his eyes to adjust before he could see anything at all. The first thing that became visible as more than a dull blur was the carbine-waving guerillas impatiently motioning the group against a wall. Revill could feel a dirt floor under his boots. One by one the faces of the Intercontinental people became recognizable again—Jennifer, Harold, Kenneth, Terry, Ray—if the white-faced, gargoyle-stiff features of the group could be called recognizable.

"You understand Spanish?" Chama's voice boomed.

Revill tried to focus upon the direction of the sound. He had no idea to whom Chama was speaking. Then his vision cleared sufficiently that he could see Chama's back as the guerilla leader bent down over a long table in the hut's center, a much more sturdy-looking table than Revill would have expected to find in such a place.

He could see Muriel upon her back on the table, strapped down tightly. Leather belts fastened her down at the ankles, knees, thighs, waist, below her breasts and across her throat. Belts also fastened her wrists through holes in the table.

"I understand," Muriel replied faintly.

"Good!" Chama said vigorously. "I want you to know why I do this. Women do not spit upon men. Rodolfo!" he said, and reached behind him without looking.

Revill saw a silvery glint as a guerilla stepped up behind Chama and placed something in his back-stretched hand. For a heart-stopping instant Revill thought it was a knife, but then he saw that it was something larger and heavier. Then two more of Chama's men moved in beside Muriel's head and with dirty-gloved hands and thumbs forced her mouth open. Chama reached into the straining mouth with the pliers handed to him a moment before and pulled at a front-centered tooth with brutal force. With a sickehing sound it came loose and he flung the tooth with its bloody root against the far wall.

Muriel shrieked as her entire body bucked upward

against the unyielding straps. Chama laughed, his eyes bulging hideously while he probed inside her mouth again. Muriel screamed, a prolonged, full-throated sound of agony. Saliva and blood dribbled down from the corners of her mouth.

"Try spitting after I've finished with you!" Chama growled. He pulled another tooth.

Revill shuddered, and stole a glance at his companions. Jennifer and Terry showed a flicker of some emotion he couldn't identify, but the others, including Ray Willoughby, wore glazed masks. As indeed, he realized suddenly, his own face must be.

Time after time Chama inserted the pliers into Muriel's battered, bleeding mouth and pulled another tooth. When she tried to keep her mouth closed against the gloved hands forcing it open, Chama callously rapped the handle of the pliers against her lips until her mouth opened again. Muriel's shrieks grew fainter until they blended into a long, continuous wail.

Chama stepped away from the table, finally, and returned the bloody pliers to the donor. He bent down again and studied Muriel's mouth. Her breath was coming in gasps that racked her whole body. "Try spitting now, *puta!*" Chama shouted. He turned away, apparently satisfied. Three men removed the straps confining Muriel to the table. She didn't move.

Two of the men grasped her by the shoulders and sat her up on the table as she moaned. Her head lolled, but she was conscious. Her mouth gaped open, revealing through its crimson dribblings that Chama had pulled every other tooth, both upper and lower. He had done it with almost surgical precision so that upper and lower teeth never met in the ruined mouth.

The men slid Muriel from the table. She was a rag doll in their hands. Her lower lip was already beginning to swell from the continual pressure of the pliers' handle against it. There was a large, dark-stained area at the crotch of her clothing.

The guerillas dragged her across the room with her heels scraping. They dropped her at the end of the line of standing prisoners. She fell to the earthen floor with a soft plopping sound.

None of the prisoners looked down at her.

Eyes straight ahead, they stared at the far wall.

6

David McCarter emerged from the phone booth at the Galeao Airport in Rio de Janeiro and nodded to Gary Manning. "He'll meet us at his place," he said. "It's a twenty-kilometer cab ride into town. Runs up the bloody expenses a bit. If our flight had come into Santos Dumont Airport we'd have saved cab fare."

Manning took in as much of the city as he could during the ride into town. Brilliant sunshine still somehow didn't seem to dissipate entirely a lazy layer in the upper atmosphere. The streets were broad and colorful, and the people seemed cheerful.

When they left the cab, they walked an additional five blocks to their destination. McCarter knocked three times upon a door that was almost flush with the sidewalk in a building that had not been built the day before yesterday. The area consisted of light industry and small wholesalers.

Manning found himself looking down upon a five-foot three, jaunty-looking, beret-wearing little man who had unlocked his door to them. "Gary, this is Sweetie-Pie," McCarter introduced them. "Who is not as ineffectual as he looks." He spoke in French, a stilted, academic French.

"Don't mind his appalling sense of humor," Gary said in the colloquial accent of his native Montreal.

He shook hands. "We always feel we need to warn people that David is about two signatures away from being committed."

"You're a Canuck, yes?" Sweetie-Pie rasped in a surprising bass. "Oh, you don't need to warn me about The Mixmaster. I've been with him a couple of times when I'd have spread shit on him if I'd had any handy." The little man's French was Parisian argot.

Gary smiled. He had noticed the door to Sweetie-Pie's place of business when he had passed through it. Wood on both sides with a steel plate sandwiched between. As a professional consultant specializing in terrorist protection, Gary noticed such things.

"You're here to socialize, right?" Sweetie-Pie was saying to McCarter. "To take me out for the night life tonight and buy me a drink or three?"

"Exactly," David replied. "But since we're here, why don't you show Gary your magic lantern show?"

The little man removed a ring of keys from his pocket and walked to the far wall. He inserted a key in an almost invisible keyhole, then moved sideways a door hung on a track. Before it was moved it was so flush to the wall as to be even more invisible. Gary glimpsed the glimmer of steel in the wooden sandwich of this door, too.

The room into which Sweetie-Pie led them, after closing the secret door behind them, was long and narrow. There were no windows. The walls were lined with high shelves beneath which were closed-door low cabinets. Neatly arrayed and labeled on the shelves were the leading handguns of the world. Gary eyed them closely: seemingly all makes and calibers.

To the trained eye most had obviously been used, but they had been worked over and reconditioned to an almost new appearance. At the far end of the room were cartons and bins of spare parts.

"Very nice," Gary approved. "*Very* nice." He reached up and removed from a shelf a Smith & Wesson Model 59 which he balanced in his palm.

"Notice the four-inch barrel," Sweetie-Pie said immediately, "9mm caliber, fourteen-shot capacity, weight twenty-seven ounces."

"Always the salesman," McCarter said. He spoke to Gary in English. "I'd been thinking we should have six of this and half a dozen of that, but perhaps we should have a mix? Not appear quite so—ahh—organized?"

"I agree," Gary said. He placed two of the Smith & Wesson Model 59s upon a small table.

"That Beretta's a comfortable gun," Sweetie-Pie said. "It's the 951 model, 9mm Luger, four-and-a-half-inch barrel, cross-bolt safety, eight shots, thirty-one ounces."

McCarter added two Berettas to Manning's Smith & Wessons.

"If you want to keep it down to one-caliber ammo," Sweetie-Pie continued, "there's the French 9mm 1950 Automatic, similar to the Colt .45. It's a nine-shot—"

"Sweetie-Pie," McCarter said reproachfully. "It's also a distressing weapon that fires in the semi-automatic mode only."

"How could I have forgotten that?" Sweetie Pie admonished himself. He took down an undistinguished-looking pistol and held it out to Gary. "The

MAB P-15. Used by the French armed forces and also sold commercially around the globe. Nine-millimeter Parabellum. Six-inch barrel. Fifteen-shot magazine. Two and a half pounds.''

"That's his nationalistic nature showing, Gary," McCarter said. "Sweetie-Pie doesn't consider he's made a sale unless he includes something French made."

Gary sighted down the barrel. "I like that fifteen-shot magazine," he said. "It's comforting to think of the other guy needing to reload before you do." He added two of the P-15s to the growing accumulation upon the table.

"How about stutterers, Sweetie-Pie?" McCarter asked.

The little man took out his keys again and un-locked two waist-high, side-by-side cabinets. Gary could see carbines, automatic rifles, machine guns, and submachine guns. Sweetie-Pie straightened up with a submachine gun in each hand, one of which he handed to McCarter and the other to Manning.

"That one—" Sweetie-Pie said, pointing to the one in Gary's hands "—is also 9mm Parabellum. The barrel is only 9.05 inches. The loaded weight is less than nine and a half pounds. The—"

Gary gave him back the weapon. "It's also French made," he said interrupting the sales pitch, "has a thirty-two round magazine, and fires in the auto-matic mode only. Really, Sweetie-Pie."

The little man smiled. "Just testing," he said.

McCarter brandished the Uzi that Sweetie-Pie had handed him. "This is much better," he said. "This is what I call a practical, all-purpose weapon. How many do you think we should have, Gary?"

Manning had returned to the top shelves where he was browsing. "I'd say three," he said absently. "But check Rafael's shopping list." He took down a Ruger Super Blackhawk .44 Magnum and turned it over and over in his hands.

McCarter removed a slip of paper from his wallet. "Three it is," he said after scanning it quickly. He added two more Uzi submachine guns to the pile of weapons on the table. Sweetie-Pie was stacking up boxes of ammunition.

"One carbine," McCarter read from his list. He reached down into a cabinet and picked one up, noticing for the first time what Gary was doing. "What d'you think you could do with that bloody thing?" he asked. "The barrel must be eight inches."

"Not quite," Gary returned.

"You'd still be a day and a half getting it out of your belt."

"Maybe, but the gun will reach out and get you something when just about anything else you can name is plowing up dirt." Gary added the Ruger to the pile.

Sweetie-Pie had been studying the accumulation. "Where's the war?" he asked. "Or are you boys going to start one, maybe?"

"Don't forget the ammo for the Ruger," David advised him. "How much for the lot, Sweetie?"

"What about flares?" the little man inquired. "Grenades? Launchers? Mortars? Rockets?"

"No rockets," Manning said. "It's a little more expensive to fire a rocket at a man than it is a round from a carbine. You need a good-sized target for a rocket."

"But sprinkle in a few of the others you mentioned,'' McCarter decided. ''There's no one like Sweetie-Pie set up like a mom-and-pop grocery out there. How much for the lot, Sweetie?''

The little man looked at him thoughtfully, looked at Gary, then looked at the stacks of weapons to which he had added the most recently mentioned items. ''At my usual rate, ninety-five hundred,'' he said. ''But since you're an old and valued customer I'll knock off ten percent.''

''Add in a little plastique for our boy here,'' McCarter said, gesturing toward Manning. ''He's the Wizard of Id with the stuff. He'll destroy a mannequin in a shop window without blowing the glass out onto the street.'' David was unbuckling his belt. He half-masted his slacks, pulled up his shirt, and removed a money belt from around his waist.

After opening it, he counted large-numbered bills down upon the table with the speed-dazzling efficiency of a Las Vegas craps dealer. He stopped, then added three more bills. ''There you are, Sweetie,'' he said. ''I rounded it off to nine thousand, including the plastique.''

The little man picked up the money from the table, but the look of surprise on his face quickly turned to suspicion. ''What the hell's going on, McCarter?'' he demanded. ''You never yet paid me my asking price.''

''We don't have time to shop around,'' McCarter answered. ''It's as simple as that why we have to submit to your holdup scheme.'' He was stuffing in his shirttails. ''Would you rather fly us in with the stuff tonight or wait until morning?''

''Ah-hah!'' Sweetie-Pie exclaimed triumphantly.

He threw the cash down upon the table, then grabbed for it when it started to slide off. "How come *that* particular subject never happened to come up before?"

"Be reasonable, Sweetie," David said in his most reasonable tone. "We can't lug this stuff across borders. That's how *you* keep your mustard pickle on the table. You drop us off with it—tonight would be nice—and then you're off and away."

"How far?"

"A thousand miles, give or take a couple hundred."

"Where?"

"Paraguay. An hour inside its northern border."

The little man shook his head. "Negative, McCarter. Stroessner's one dictator who scares me."

"Dictator?" McCarter asked innocently. "Didn't I read somewhere he was elected in '58, '63, '68, '73, and '78?"

"Yeah, and the Pope's Presbyterian," Sweetie-Pie snorted. "Who counted the votes? Who manned the ballot boxes?" He shook his head again. "I'm telling you the man scares me."

"Scares *you*?" McCarter looked at Manning. "Listen to that propaganda, will you, Gary? Why, Sweetie-Pie Sazerac is famous in the munitions game because he's the only dealer who ever fired his own weapons in anger."

"I'm not buying *that* propaganda," the little man growled. Gary reached casually for the money on the table. Sweetie-Pie picked up the money and hefted it in his hand. "Who pays for the fuel?" he demanded.

"We do," McCarter said.

"Okay. I'll have the goods here packed for you by the time we come back from having that drink or three. Three crates sound about right?"

"Make it four," David said. "None of them too heavy."

Gary looked at him in surprise before he remembered. "How's your shoulder, David?"

"Perfect."

"What happened to his shoulder?" Sweetie-Pie wanted to know.

"A pigeon kicked it," McCarter replied before Manning could say anything.

The little man snorted, then led the way back to the front of his place of business.

7

Rafael led the way to customs at the Presidente General Stroessner Aeropuerto in Asunción. The terminal, although well kept up, was almost a miniature of the world's great international airports. "Let me do the talking," he said to Yak and KO.

The customs inspector examined the passports Rafael handed over, the passports that had been hand-delivered to Rafael from Mack Bolan before the group left Miami. "Do you have need of a guide?" the inspector asked while he perfunctorily checked passport photos against the individuals standing before him. "I can arrange it."

"No, thanks," Rafael said. "The professor's friends at the university—" he nodded toward Yak "—are taking care of all of that for us. We appreciate your offer, most sincerely, but we would not wish to appear ungrateful in the eyes of the professor's colleagues."

The inspector bowed respectfully to Yak. "Which are the professor's bags?" he asked. Yak pointed out two bags, and the inspector marked them at once with an x within a circle. Lowering the chalk in his hand, he waited while Rafael and KO opened their bags. He flipped through them cursorily, closed the bags, and applied his chalk to them as well.

"If you have need of additional information about flights, there is a downtown office on Independencia Nacional," the customs inspector said.

"I know," Rafael returned. "Thank you for your courtesy."

They walked out into the terminal lobby after Rafael signaled a waiting porter to stack the bags on a wheeled cart. "That was easy," KO remarked.

"Thanks to the professor here," Rafael grinned. "Nowhere is education honored more than in a country which has very little of it."

"I see now why you repacked the bags on the flight down," Yak said.

Rafael nodded. "The walkie-talkies and a few other little goodies are in your bags now."

"What if the inspector had been a *fútbol* fan and not an education buff?" KO demanded.

"Yes, I'm sure you had an alternate story concocted," Yak agreed.

"Merely that you were a physicist at General Stroessner's Scientific Institute and were hurrying back to bring word of a breakthrough in long-distance communications."

"A true storyteller," KO said to Yak with a laugh.

"You can see why he is such a devil with the ladies," Yak responded.

The porter obtained a taxi for them. It was an elderly Chrysler whose original green paint had faded to a bilious celery color. "Probably gets about four miles to the gallon," KO said as they boarded it after watching the porter place their luggage into the cab's cavernous trunk. Rafael tipped him.

"Los Miradores Hotel," Rafael said to the driver.

He settled into the back seat with the others. "Not the best, but you will learn that it has some hidden advantages."

"How far into town?" Yak inquired.

"About seven miles. The airport is closer to the center of town than most international airports because of the comparative absence of skyscrapers."

"What now?" KO wanted to know.

"Yak goes to see his friends to find out if there have been any further developments on the forced-down hostage plane. I wouldn't use the telephone if I were you, Yak. KO, I want you to ask at the hotel desk for an English-speaking guide to show you the sights of the city in a private car, a cab if necessary."

"It hardly sounds as if I have much to contribute here," KO said. He said it quietly, but it was obvious he felt hurt.

"Don't jump to conclusions too quickly," Rafael said sharply. "Let the driver take you wherever he wants to, which will probably include the homes of a couple of his cousins selling silver artifacts or leather wear in their kitchens. Buddy up to him, KO. Tip him too much. Get his telephone number so we can call him any time we need transportation within the city limits. It will be a lot better than taking one of the hotel's cabs, which more than likely will be driven by Stroessner's secret police."

"What will you be doing, Rafael?" Yak inquired.

"I'll be paddling my canoe around town trying to line up land transportation for us to Concepción. Unless Yak's friends end up steering us in another direction."

"You mean buying transportation?" KO asked.

"I doubt it. That would be asking for three weeks' worth of paperwork."

"Liberating the transportation?" Yak suggested.

"It may·come to that. Yes, Yak, you could end up as the undocumented truck owner ferrying his employees to the site of his archaeological dig."

The cab pulled up in front of the Los Miradores Hotel.

8

Yakov Katzenelenbogen sat back in the comfortable leather armchair in the small conference room on the university campus and held out his sherry glass to his host to be topped up. He had been introduced in turn to a Thierry Tulasne, an Arturo Gonzalez, and a Remo Consolo. His host's name was Jaime Middleton. Yak had been introduced as Paul Cartier, the name on the passport freshly supplied to him from Mack Bolan's headquarters.

"Paul has been field leader on several interesting digs in the Middle East," Middleton was saying as he poured sherry for the others. He was a large, bearded man. Despite his last name, it was obvious he had been Spanish for two or three generations, although the conversation was in English. "I was fortunate enough to be with him on a couple of them."

"Have you anything in prospect there now?" Gonzalez asked. He held out his glass again for Middleton's decanter.

"Unfortunately, no," Yak replied. "I have a promising situation in Egypt, but it's going to have to await better political and personal relationships in the area."

"We don't have even that excuse," Tulasne

sighed. "But we just can't get the funding. The government has other priorities."

"It's true in a lot of countries. But I should add a disclaimer to Jaime's remark a moment ago. I'm not a pioneer in the sense that a Middleton—" he nodded toward the host "—or a Tulasne, a Gonzalez, or a Consolo, whose names I recognize from the literature, is a pioneer." He bowed in turn from his sitting position to each of the men in turn, and they returned the nods, obviously pleased at the recognition.

"I consider myself a scavenger," Yak continued. "My contribution has been principally to return to established but abandoned digs and try to find artifacts overlooked due to time pressure on the original excavation."

"And occasionally to correct errors in judgment made under that same time pressure," Middleton added.

"There is never enough time on a dig to get it all right," Yak said in a deprecating tone.

"Do you have any governmental problems here other than financing?" he went on after a moment's silence. He wanted these men talking about local political conditions.

"Red tape," Consolo said promptly. "It can be as bad as acquiring a grant."

"Worse, sometimes," Gonzalez said.

"The red tape is worse," Consolo insisted. Even an application made to excavate Indian burial mounds in the interior—"

"In which Remo is especially interested," Middleton broke in.

Consolo nodded before he continued "—runs into

oversight and neglect at every government level. Every petty little bureaucrat jumps to the conclusion we're digging for gold and silver. When he decides it's too risky to try to cut himself in on the gravy train, he's determined no one else shall experience the good fortune he can't manufacture for himself. I have gone hoarse trying to explain to the idiots in government that we are dealing with a *primitive* people here. On this coastal plain the Indians had no use for gold or silver except in minute quantities for ornamentation."

"Everyone thinks of the Mayans and the Aztecs when he sees an application for a dig," Jaime Middleton agreed. "I have a fresh rejection myself acquired after eighteen months of fruitless pleading."

"And Jaime is better connected in local political circles than any of us," Tulasne added.

Yak felt the first faint stirring of inspiration. "May I see the form your applications are required to take here?" he asked Middleton. "Red tape is red tape the world over, but once in a while a troublesome point anticipated is a point that can be dealt with by foreknowledge."

Middleton rose from his chair and went to a desk in a corner of the room. "The rejection is so fresh I haven't transferred it to my own files," he explained. He handed Yak a thick sheaf of papers that had been bludgeoned by bureaucratic stamps. Yak glanced quickly at the top two sheets, then sat with the packet in his lap. Rafael with his bird-dog instinct and quickly established rapport with the seamier side of life in a large city might well be able to do something with this.

"Have you had any news of digs in progress?" Tulasne asked.

Yak talked for half an hour, dredging up what he could recall from his recent reading in the journals. The men sat forward in their chairs, eager for crumbs of the cake which they were denied locally. Finally, Yak glanced at his watch. "I'm afraid, gentlemen—"

"Yes," Middleton said at once. "We're imposing upon what I'm sure is your limited time."

The other men rose and approached Yak's chair, where they expressed their appreciation for his sharing of news. They departed one by one until Yak and Middleton were alone.

"I know you, Yakov," Middleton said quietly then. "You're here about that business you phoned me about, aren't you? I can tell you that it has turned the police and the army upside down. They are turning over all stones. I don't understand it, the provocation, I mean. I wouldn't have thought there was a guerilla group extant with enough courage to make a direct challenge like that to the general."

"There's always the chance of outside reinforcement," Yak said. "Is it still true that it's in the area of Concepción that they are looking?"

"Yes. It's not easy for them. The entire army numbers only twelve and a half thousand men, and there is a small garrison in every crossroads village to keep the general's thumb on local situations. Only good-sized cities have a police force, and they, of course, are paramilitary. I should tell you, Yakov, that in the current situation it would be very difficult for even someone as skilled in the art of semi-invisibility as you to get near the area without being stopped for questioning. Given the general's mood, it could be dangerous, very dangerous.''

Yak held out the packet of papers representing a failed presentation for an archaeological dig. ''Would you happen to have in your old files, Jaime, a packet such as this for a dig that was approved and completed?''

''Why, yes, but I don't see—''

''I have a friend who can lift off stamps and signatures and apply them to a fresh application which I will prepare for a dig in the jungle around Concepción. Which army sergeant would question it?''

Middleton smiled. ''Which, indeed? Let's walk across the campus to my office and you can have such an approved application plus blank forms.'' His smile vanished. ''But it will still be dangerous, Yakov. Make no mistake about it. With anyone other than you I would feel myself forced to say no.''

Yak finished off his sherry and they departed from the conference room.

9

Sweetie-Pie's VW bumped down the side road, which had lost its macadam after the first hundred meters. They had driven through one of Rio's sudden showers, and the warm black night enveloping them felt like damp velvet.

The dirt road swung toward the left, and the VW came to a stop with its bumper against a barbwire fence. The little Frenchman got out and moved a section of the fence aside, enough to permit him to drive through. David McCarter and Gary Manning could see a grassy field in the VW's headlights, a low, undulating greensward that passed beyond the scope of the lights.

The VW shot across the field until a large, gray building loomed up in front of them. It looked to Gary like a barn. Sweetie-Pie parked the VW and they all climbed out. McCarter sauntered toward the middle of the field, whistling softly under his breath. "Goddam!" he said finally. He pointed ahead of them. "That's our runway, and I'll guarantee you Sweetie might have fifteen yards clearance before he runs out of room, but he doesn't have twenty. This field is a tight overcoat."

A grating sound behind them turned their heads around. The Frenchman had his shoulder against a sliding door which he was moving to one side on well-oiled rollers. They hurried to help him. Manning's eyes gradually adjusted to the deeper darkness of the interior until he was able to make out the details of a well-appointed hangar, complete with row upon row of pegboards laden with all manner of tools.

His gaze focused upon the white bulk of a twin-engine, trim-looking airplane with bright red crosses painted upon its fuselage and tail assembly. "An ambulance plane!" he exclaimed.

"What better passport?" McCarter asked with a grin. "And it's legitimate. It's Sweetie's visible means of support. Not his money-maker. The munitions take care of that. But there's probably no tower controller in any large city in the Southern Hemisphere who hasn't seen Monsieur Sazerac's Beechcraft Baron fly in on some errand of mercy. Nobody ever takes a second look."

The Frenchman had already entered the plane via the door above the wing. To one side, alongside the baggage compartment, were four crates. "Ours?" Gary asked.

"Ours," David confirmed. He walked to the side of the plane and rapped his knuckles upon the fuselage. "Open up, Sweetie."

The luggage-compartment door swung to one side and McCarter bent down to the first crate. Manning moved him to one side. "I'll handle this," he said. "It won't do your shoulder a bit of good." David McCarter's shoulder had intercepted a bullet during their last mission.

Gary found the crates heavy but manageable. Once stowed away, he went back out to the VW for their bags. Sweetie-Pie was descending from the wing. "Give me a hand," he said. "No sense firing up the tractor when I've got two horses like you around."

Together they pushed the Beechcraft out onto the field. It rolled easily once under way. Sweetie-Pie climbed back up into the cockpit. "All aboard," David said to Gary. He led the way, stepping up to enter, then turning right into the body of the aircraft. Gary, following, looked around at two hospital beds and all manner of medical apparatus lashed to the walls of what would ordinarily have been a roomy cabin. The windows, which ordinarily afforded panoramic visibility, were shrouded by white vinyl coverings.

"What about runway lights?" Gary asked.

David shook his head. "Sweetie's got a big halogen spotlight in the plane's nose, and he knows every weed on the field."

"He sure as hell won't know every weed where we land!" Gary declared.

David raised his voice as the engines started up. "Sweetie lands at dawn," he shouted. "Always. It's his trademark." He was looking around the cabin area. "This is one beautiful piece of machinery. It's the E-55 model, with the two hundred and eighty-five horsepower Continental engines. Top speed is a bit less than two fifty, but the range is twelve hundred miles. And it carries a useful load of two tons."

"Quite an investment," Gary said.

"Not for Sweetie. The next jump upward in plane size would move him into a more visible situation he doesn't care for. Taxes, and all that. He could afford a bloody 747, but he keeps a low profile. So he sticks with the Baron.''

''What's his background?''

''Sweetie-Pie Sazerac is a money-making machine. Midas, Croesus, all those types were pikers compared to him. But once he was a patriot. He found himself in Algeria with the OAS, and it cured him. He wasn't a *colon* or an army right-winger, and he got tired of hearing and seeing Algerian nationalists' testicles crushed. He got himself transferred to the Quartermaster Corps, and eighteen months later the Quartermaster General found out Sweetie was knocking down more than the general was. They threw his ass right off the continent.''

''You trust him?''

''Yes,'' David said with a smile. ''When it is me involved, Sweetie's the type who, once he crosses an invisible line, is in an affair until the last rocket's fired. Besides, we have a special relationship that goes 'way back. Meantime—'' he raised his voice again as the engines accelerated ''—I'll go up in the jump seat and watch the instruments to make sure he doesn't forget something.''

Gary Manning settled himself into a seat and buckled himself in. He felt the plane taxi out to the end of the runway. A powerful beam of light came on in the nose of the plane, illuminating their takeoff run across the bumpy grass. Then the bumpiness smoothed, and the Baron swooped upward, crossing a highway and then a river. It banked to the left, the nose-light went off, and the night closed in around them completely.

10

Keio Ohara stood in the print shop, casually examining displayed business cards in Spanish he couldn't understand. Ten yards to the rear of the shop, Rafael and the printer spoke earnestly in Spanish, Yak's archaeological forms spread out on the counter between them. The printer was nodding his head in agreement. KO couldn't understand what they were saying.

The front door opened and a tall man in a tan suit strode in. Something KO understood perfectly was the outline of a shoulder holster under the newcomer's jacket as he made his way rapidly toward the rear of the store. That, and the terrified look on the face of the printer, caused KO to start moving noiselessly toward the trio.

Yak's forged passport was also on the counter. The tall man picked it up. He also reached across the counter and snatched from the printer's unnerved hand the archaeological papers he had instinctively grabbed up. "What need have tourists of printing, Gomez?" the tall man asked. He spoke with the careless confidence of authority.

Again, KO didn't understand. He was only a yard behind the tall man, still unnoticed. "Now," Rafael said to KO in English. "I'll check outside and make sure he's come alone."

The tall man turned his head to look at Rafael, uncertain about the English. KO understood everything now. He reached out and tapped the tall man on the shoulder. The man whirled, grabbing for the gun in his holster, but then he slowed when he saw KO's face. KO was smiling at him, a large, bland Oriental smile.

The man started to relax just as KO smashed the heel of his right palm against the side of the man's nose, just at the top of his cheek. The crunch of the breaking bone could be heard plainly. The tremendous force of the plow popped the man's left eye from its socket. It dangled from its stalk on his cheek like a small, unripened grape.

Passport and papers fell to the floor. The man's head had flown off to the side. KO intercepted the path of its movement with a driving left hook to the chin. The man crashed into the counter. KO put his shoulder and arm into a palm smash that landed an inch above the man's belt buckle. He doubled up and started to fall forward. KO met the oncoming face with a sharply upraised knee, and the man went over backward. His face a ruined red mask. Only seconds had elapsed since the man reached for his holster.

Rafael hadn't stayed to observe the carnage. He was already at the door of the shop, checking the street. He returned briskly to the rear of the shop, sparing only a glance at KO's victim. "Apparently alone," he said to KO.

He turned to the printer. "What was that about?" he demanded.

The printer was having difficulty in swallowing. "He is—he's the gov-government informer on this block," he stammered. "But he's n-never here at this time of the afternoon. He's—he's always at the house of the women.''

Rafael snorted. He knelt down and picked up the passport and papers. While on one knee, he restored the dangling eyeball to its socket and gently lodged it under the eyelid. He rose and handed the man the papers and passport. "Get this done," he said. "Transferred signatures, too. I'll be back for it."

"But I'll—I'll go to jail!" The printer was almost gibbering. "If they don't kill me! He's—he's from the s-secret police! I know you came well-recommended, but—"

Rafael gave him an intimidating smile. "Don't worry about this one. Get the job done. Come on, KO."

KO reached down with three hooked fingers for the carotid artery in the neck of the man on the floor. "Not here," Rafael said in English. "Not yet. We'll carry him out." He switched to Spanish again. "Where is this whorehouse?" he asked the printer.

The printer stared at him blankly. "This—?"

"You said he went there every afternoon."

"Oh. Yes. Of course. Certainly." He raised a trembling hand to point toward his rear door. "Two blocks down that way. Next to the flower shop. On the second floor."

Rafael and KO reached down and picked up the man and supported him between them. They carried him to the rear door with his legs dangling. The printer followed, bleating, ready to slam and bolt the door behind them.

"If you're asked," Rafael said in temporary farewell, "he never came here today. You never saw him.

He must have been delayed if he told anyone he was coming. You understand?''

The printer nodded wordlessly.

Rafael and KO walked through an alley with their burden. "Very far?" KO asked when they reached the street. Again he hadn't understood the interchange between Rafael and the printer.

"Two blocks," Rafael grunted. They walked in silence then, carrying the man with their hands under his arms high enough so his feet dragged just slightly. "Upstairs," Rafael said when he saw the flower shop. "We must not be in as good shape as we'd like to think," he said at the top of the stairs after knocking upon the door. His face was florid and sweaty. KO was breathing hard.

A slot in the door opened, and a wizened, elderly Chinese face appeared. "Good afternoon, *princesa*," Rafael said, switching to Spanish again. "We have here one drunk and two men ready for business." He handed a twenty-dollar U.S. bill through the slot.

The old woman opened the door, and they moved inside with their burden. Three girls were seated in an anteroom. They looked up curiously. "Get me a towel, O Light of My Life," Rafael said to the nearest one. He and KO steered the man between them to an armchair. Rafael supported the head in an upright position until the girl returned with a towel. He placed it under the bloody head. "One drink too many today," he said to the girl. "He had a bad fall."

"If he's sick, Chen Yi will make you pay," the girl warned.

The man in the chair stirred, muttered something unintelligible, then went limp again.

Rafael reached out and patted a plump hip through the thin camisolelike garment the girl was wearing. "You look like you know how to gallop," he told the girl. Arm around her, he turned to look inquiringly toward KO.

"I'll stay here," KO said hastily. "In case—"

"He's no problem," Rafael said.

"There's always a chance."

"Then—" Rafael said. He moved toward the chair. The Chinese proprietress had disappeared. Rafael bent down over the chair, and KO, anticipating, moved closer so that his bulk blocked the view of the girls. "They saw him move," Rafael said in a conversational tone to KO. "They know he was alive when we brought him in here."

He removed a small object from a pocket that looked like a cigarette lighter. He applied it to the nape of the inanimate neck and squeezed a tiny trigger. There was a slight click as a slender needle plunged deeply into the nape. Only the tiniest dot of blood showed when Rafael removed the plunger-activated device. The eyeball of the good eye rolled upward until the white showed.

Rafael stepped back, turned, and led the girl down the hallway.

He returned in fifteen minutes humming to himself.

He looked at KO, seated in a chair. "You could still—"

"No, I couldn't," KO said emphatically. "And I don't see how you could, either."

The proprietress had reappeared. "We'll send a cab for that one," Rafael said to her. "*Adios, mama.*" He led the way out. On the stairs, he turned to look at KO. "If the guy talked about going to the printer's, when they find him here they'll think he stopped off here first."

"If he didn't follow us from the hotel."

"No, the printer said that block was his territory. Besides, we weren't meant to be that unlucky."

They resumed their way down the stairs to the street.

11

The cages were ten by six by eight. Contained inside one of the huts, they consisted of iron bars running from the top of the cage into the hard earth. Rough boards for siding were surprisingly effective in muffling conversation from the cages on either side. There were two inmates to a cage, in quarters so close that almost any uncontrolled movement resulted in involuntary contact and additionally frayed nerves. The fetid odor inside the hut itself hung over the cages like the foul breath of a swamp.

Ian Revill's cage partner had introduced himself as Terry Conrad from Jersey City. He was slender, about thirty-two years, and an intense-looking man. He had facial bruises and his eyeglass frames were broken at one temple, but clumsily bound together with thread unraveled from a handkerchief. Revill couldn't decide if the warped glasses had given Conrad's face a misshapen appearance or if a cheekbone had actually been fractured.

During their second day together in the cage Conrad had produced a battered spoon and a suggestion. "The bars are rusted," he said. "We might not have to do much diggin' to expose the ends and bend them outward." He spoke with a hot-eyed vehemence that made Revill uneasy and caused him to hesitate. "We could get away from these bastards,'' Conrad insisted.

Get away, Revill wondered. Out of the cage, possibly. Out of the hut, less likely. Off the island, far less likely. And through the surrounding jungle, impossible. But he hadn't wanted to blunt the initiative of Conrad, who as nearly as Revill could tell from his brief contacts with the other hostages, alone retained a semblance of spirit.

They had talked it over, and decided to dig each night from nine to midnight, as closely as they could judge it. Revill's Rolex had been confiscated by Chama. Conrad's had long since disappeared among the Bolivian guerillas. From nine to midnight they could take advantage of whatever noise the guerillas themselves made and whatever sounds came from the adjoining cages. After midnight the entire camp settled into a stillness that magnified a rat's passage into the sound of a horse's trot.

Last night Conrad had dug away at the earth packed around a bar at the rear of the cell while Revill sat at the front talking steadily to conceal or disguise the sound of Conrad's spoon-scraping. Loose earth piled upon Conrad's shirt was moved to the front of the cage where Revill spread it thinly in the corners and trod it down. He was surprised at how much the talking wearied him, and how difficult it was to keep a flow going. The final thirty minutes he had ended up reciting the rules of rugby.

Tonight Revill was digging and Conrad was talking. He described himself as a commercial photographer who had come to South America to build up portfolio credits and had stayed ''even though he was

goddam sick of art directors back at headquarters
who ripped off his good ideas.'' Revill thought that
Terry Conrad must be the youngest of the entire
group.

Conrad had observed Revill's icy hatred of
Chama, and he admired Revill's control in not showing it. "I couldn't keep from showin' the fuckers
how I felt about 'em,'' he was saying now, repeating
himself as he often did. "We had one Bolivian ape
back there made Chama seem like a schoolgirl.
Always messin' with people's heads. Never knew his
name. When the women were around, we called him
The Turkey. We called him somethin' else when they
weren't.''

Revill slid his dirt-laden shirt down between their
bodies to Conrad who began spreading it and tread-
ing it down. Revill returned to his digging while Conrad again stretched out on the hard ground and
resumed talking.

"He really got us all screwed up in our heads,''
Conrad said, and Revill knew he was again speaking
of The Turkey. "How many six-hour lectures on dia-
lectical materialism can you stand before you flake
out? But it was the physical stuff that broke us down.
The Turkey had a lot of cute tricks aimed at playin'
us off against each other. Gettin' us mad at each
other. Just about insane mad. He had one gimmick
that, well—''

Conrad half-rolled onto his side and peered
through the cage's blackness at the almost invisible
Revill. "They'd strip you down, see? Blindfold you,
gag you, an' push into a room you see is pitch black
just before they put on the blindfold. They spread-

eagle you on your back on a table with arms and legs fastened to the four corners. An' then you wait. Wait for pain. What and when is all that's in your mind. The first time I like went out've my mind waitin' for the boilin' oil or whatever. But then The Turkey pulled a switch.''

"Hold it down," Revill said as Conrad's voice rose in intensity.

"Yeah, yeah. Or they'd strap you to a wall, ankles, wrists and neck. Eventually you hear 'em bringing in someone else, and the someone else is tied against you belly-to-belly. You can't see an' you can't talk, right? But it still takes maybe only forty-five seconds to filter through to you that the person up against you is a naked female.''

Conrad spat as though his throat had thickened up. "So there you are, right? Scared shitless about what's next, but aware of the intense sexuality of it all. And the woman doesn't know who she's with, either. Is it one of us? Or an outsider? Or one of them, playing a game. Poor Muriel and Jennifer. They'll never be the same. And Muriel was a real good-looker.''

Revill had stopped digging and turned his head to listen.

"We called it Bolivian Roulette. It's enough to make you crazy," Conrad went on, his words blurred in the rush of remembered anger. "Yes, nothing like fear, anger, humiliation and curiosity to rattle your gonads.''

"Hold it *down*!" Revill whispered as Conrad's voice rose again.

"Yeah, sure. You begin to wonder what you'll ever be able to do with a naked woman again. . . .''

No wonder these people hated each other, Revill thought. The Turkey had really learned his psychology lessons. Divide and conquer.

"One mornin' one of the young guerillas who helped arrange these games and spoke a little English started needlin' me about my masculinity. An' I blew. I really creamed the sucker. I didn't care if the world ended. For two minutes I had him prayin' for a better world. 'Course, then the wave washed over me.''

He drew a husky breath. "The bunch of 'em tromped on me for awhile, but my adrenaline was so high I wasn't hurtin' too bad. I was even kind of gigglin' to myself. But you know somethin'? That goddam Turkey even knew *that*!''

Revill had stopped digging entirely. He was motionless, stretched out on stomach and chest, listening spellbound to the torrent of words from the Jersey City photographer. "He yelled 'em off me, an' they lugged me off, away from the rest. Wasn't no cages there in Bolivia.

"So they come back for me when there's still a little daylight left outside. No adrenaline now, see? It's been drainin' all day. They lug me out there an' circle me, an' all I am is a tight asshole tryin' to keep the scared shit from runnin' down the backs of my legs. I start beggin' and pleadin' before they start in on me. *Before*, y'hear me? They laughed an' gun-butted my kidneys an' ribs an' gut. They ran up a score. Three broken ribs, pissin' blood for a month, somethin' displaced internally. But I was beggin' them *before*.'' His voice died away in a strangled rasp. When he spoke again, it was in a whisper. "I'm never gonna feel the same about myself.''

Ian Revill packed down enough loose dirt around the bar he had been digging out to leave it looking apparently undisturbed. He spread the remainder of the dirt on his shirt in a corner and walked on it for several minutes.

And meantime he tried vainly not to hear the sound of Terry Conrad, crying.

12

Rafael stared out the cab window at the narrow alleys they were passing, each of which afforded a quick glimpse of the sluggish-looking Paraná River beyond the low warehouses. He decided that the look of the area wasn't rundown, only because it hadn't amounted to much in the first place.

"I spoke to Gomez, the printer," he said to KO who was in the back seat beside him. "Nobody came to see him. And Yak picked up a message from David at American Express. They've got the stuff and they're flying it into the target area. That makes us the cow's tail."

"Cow's tail?"

"Over the fence last. Late. Tell the cabbie to stop."

KO raised his voice. "John! Right here!"

The driver turned his head and nodded, showing a cheerful smile.

Rafael and KO climbed out when the cab stopped. Rafael reached toward his pocket but KO made a negative gesture. "He's on retainer now," he said. "Come back in an hour, John." He looked at Rafael for confirmation. Rafael nodded.

They stood and watched the cab's departure. "I know I told you to buddy up to this guy," Rafael began, "but his whole family is making a living off you. I've seen the junk in Yak's suite you've bought from them."

"Not to worry," KO said. "Before we leave, I'll hold a garage sale in the lobby of the hotel." He ducked when Rafael aimed a punch at his ribs. "What are we doing here, Machiavelli?"

"That's our truck across the street."

KO stared at a dilapidated-looking flatbed with extra high sideboards. "A Ford," he commented. "Not a T. Not an A. It must be the Paleolithic model. At least the tires look all right. Do we liberate it?"

"It's on the table for discussion. The owner is a landscape gardener. When he leaves for work each day, the truck is loaded with shovels, spades, picks, rakes, you name it. It would be good cover for us. And the truck runs. I checked."

"Then why is it on the table for discussion?"

"Because the owner is Japanese."

"Ahh, so," KO said softly. "Let's go negotiate."

"Three doors up, across the street."

At the third doorway KO saw broken-in work shoes sitting on a rubber mat. He knocked, and the door opened after a moment to reveal a tiny, bald, white-bearded, prune-faced ancient who peered up at them inquiringly.

"Greetings, honored sir," KO said in Japanese. "We beseech the favor of intruding briefly upon your valuable time."

The elderly man beamed and opened his door wider.

Rafael would have walked inside except for the

steel beam of KO's arm across his chest that prevented him. "Shoes off!" KO hissed, removing his own. Rafael meekly followed his example. When he entered behind KO, his first look around showed sparse furnishings which somehow looked comfortable in their well-used simplicity. A corner of the single room was curtained off.

The elderly Japanese said something to KO. His voice sounded rusty and unused. KO responded and sat down in a straight-backed wooden chair. "He's making tea for us," he said.

Rafael frowned. "We haven't much time, KO. We—"

"Tea is the starting point of negotiations, Rafael."

Rafael shook his head, but he seated himself. He watched the preparation of the tea on a two-burner stove. It was served in tiny cups. KO and the ancient one bowed to each other over their cups, then sipped in silence.

It was only when they set their cups aside that the conversation began. Rafael listened to the lilting syllables trying to gauge the tone of the negotiations. But then he noticed that it was the elderly man who was doing most of the talking while KO listened respectfully. For the first time Rafael experienced something of the frustration he knew KO felt during long conversations in Spanish.

He was just about to remind KO of the pressure of time again when the tone of the negotiations changed. The dialogue grew sharper. It seemed to Rafael that KO's tone was expostulating. Never mind the price, KO, he almost said aloud. Cut the deal.

KO looked over at him finally. "The truck is ours," he said.

"It is?" Rafael said, astonished. "I thought—"

"Mr. Fusaka wishes no payment."

"*No* payment? What—"

"He thinks it would be better if the truck disappeared from its parking place. He will take to his bed and meditate until the truck is returned."

Rafael felt irritated. "So what if it isn't returned? How the hell do we know what we're going to run into?"

"If it's not returned," KO replied imperturbably, "when his period of meditation is over, Mr. Fusaka will report it stolen."

Rafael nodded grudgingly. "That's not a bad idea."

"And at that time he will appreciate payment. The amount he will leave up to us."

"Not bad," Rafael said thoughtfully. "It cuts him out of any responsibility. I like it. But he's a trusting soul."

Mr. Fusaka understood Rafael's tone if not his words. Beaming, he rose to his feet and presented KO with a key he removed from his work clothes. Rafael watched while KO and Mr. Fusaka clasped hands and bowed deeply. Rafael got up and attempted a similar bow. Mr. Fusaka returned it in kind. KO led the way to the door.

"What was all that preliminary conversation about?" Rafael demanded while they were pulling on their shoes after the door closed.

"He's been here thirty years," KO said. "He was in a cave on Saipan that Marine flamethrowers cleaned up. The bodies of the other men saved him. When the first wave passed, he worked his way up into the hills and stayed there. When the war ended, he said he couldn't go back to Japan as a loser. He went down to the harbor one night, swam out to a freighter and smuggled himself aboard. Got off in Noumea. Then Sydney. Then San Francisco. Then Cartagena. He stayed a couple of years in each. Then here. He asked me about Tokyo's bullet trains. He'd read about them. He asked me how much things had changed.''

"If we get out of this thing with our asses semi-intact, the least we can do is see he gets a trip back,'' Rafael said.

KO smiled. "Sometimes you show rare perception despite your brutish appearance, Rafael.''

"We'll get the truck tonight,'' Rafael said. "I'll scout out a place to keep it until we're ready to leave.''

"Which should be when?''

"I'd think before midnight.''

They waited for the return of the cab and then rode back to the Los Miradores Hotel in silence.

13

David McCarter's gaze swept the normally function-
ing instrument panel as he looked up from the flight
chart over which he had been poring as the Beechcraft bored through the night. "Pity we seem to have
thought to bring everything except hot coffee," he
said. "Sweetie, put the ship on automatic pilot and
let's change seats. There's something I want you to
look at."

When the change had been made and David had
taken up the controls, the Frenchman looked at him
inquiringly. David jerked a thumb toward the flight
chart on its clipboard and Sweetie picked it up.

"I've been over that chart until my eyes feel like
two holes burned in a blanket," McCarter resumed,
"and there are still a couple of things that defeat me.
We know that the hostages' charter plane went off
radar near Concepción, which I've marked on your
chart. It's not so surprising we've heard nothing
about the hostages, with the new lot of guerillas holding the lid on for all they're worth, but what about
the plane? The guerillas can't have destroyed it because how else are they going to move the hostages
quickly upon short notice if they make a deal? A
friend of ours has absolutely superlative pipelines for
picking up information, yet nothing has surfaced

about the present whereabouts of a twenty-six-passenger aircraft presumably grounded and un-manned.''

"Presumably," Sweetie said. "It could have crashed while being forced down. That would account for the hostages not being heard from as well.''

"Let's not even think about that," McCarter returned. "The question to ask is whether a plane that large could fly into a backwater and not attract any attention at all?''

The Frenchman had been looking at the chart. "Communications are hardly instantaneous from Concepción. But I can think of another possibility. The airport at Concepción is on the north side of the River Paraguay where the city is, but about fifteen years ago the bureaucrats decided a better place for it was on the south side of the river on land probably owned by a politician.''

He set aside the flight chart. "It was a typical bureaucratic boondoggle. There was no road from the river to the site, so they built a road. There was no ferry to the city, so they built piers and ferries. No one had bothered to take into account the fact that depending upon the season the river had a sluggishly flowing twelve-foot depth or a briskly flowing thirty feet. Low water stranded the ferries in mud. High water tore up the riverbanks and the piers, and the underpowered ferries were carried downriver with loss of life. Eventually the airfield was abandoned.''

"But you think it could still be there?" McCarter asked eagerly.

The Frenchman shrugged. "The road grew over and the ferries rotted away, but the field might still be there. Builders in jungle areas sometimes take a lesson from the Romans when they clear a space in the jungle they want to remain cleared. They sow it with salt. It doesn't prevent entirely the return of the jungle, but it inhibits it.''

"Carthage," David murmured.

"What was that?"

"Nothing. What chance would you estimate the former airfield might have of being usable?"

"Fifteen percent. Twenty, perhaps."

"Wait a minute!" David exclaimed. "If the guerillas had a use for the field, they'd keep it in shape themselves!"

"It could be worth taking a look at." The Frenchman pointed through the windshield to where a gray streak showed along the horizon. "We're coming up on Concepción. Let's change seats again. I'm going to climb so we can do a long glide over the area and make sure there's nothing disturbing in sight before I let them hear our engines."

"What about gliding all the way in? No engine noise? This Beechcraft handles beautifully, Sweetie."

"First a look, McCarter. Then we can decide."

David had slipped on the automatic pilot and was rising from the pilot's seat when another thought struck him. "Sweetie? If the charter plane is there, there's bound to be an armed guard. The guerillas wouldn't leave it by itself if they expected to use it again."

"So?"

"So do you have any loose armament aboard this battleship, or should Gary and I open up one of the crates?"

"There's a locker inside under the lashed-up stretchers where you'll find what you need."

"That's what I like about you French boy scouts, Sweetie. Always prepared."

McCarter turned back to the cabin. Gary Manning was sleeping on one of the hospital cots, strapped down by his belt to protect himself against any sudden movement of the Baron. David seized a foot and shook it. Manning's waking was instantaneous. "What's up?" he demanded.

McCarter explained while he found the locker the Frenchman had described. Neatly sealed in plastic pouches, he found four of the same MAB P-15 pistols that seemed to be the Frenchman's favorite handgun. He broke the seals on two of them, handed one to Manning, and placed a box of 9mm Parabellum cartridges on the cot between them. In silence they loaded the fifteen-round magazines.

After a moment's thought David opened up and loaded another pistol. "Might as well give Sweetie a little personal backup," he explained.

He placed an extra box of ammunition in a jacket pocket and went back to the front of the plane. Manning followed him. He placed the extra pistol alongside Sweetie-Pie who looked at it and nodded casually.

McCarter looked down over the Frenchman's shoulder at the gauges. "Almost eighteen thousand feet," he said over his shoulder to Manning. The Beechcraft was bathed in a faint pink glow but below them was pitch blackness.

Manning instinctively grabbed for something to hold onto as the engine sound suddenly ceased.

"Sweetie's gliding in to try to give us a look," Mc-Carter said. His voice sounded loud in the silence.

"Regular airport first, if possible," Sweetie-Pie said. "To try to spot unusual activity." The Beech-craft glided onward. The Frenchman was looking at his watch. "Should be coming up," he said. "Should be—"

"There!" Manning exclaimed. He pointed toward the left.

"Concepción," Sweetie-Pie agreed. He altered course slightly.

"They must be using an automobile battery for a power plant," McCarter grumbled, studying the scattered pinpoints of light below them. "How're you going to find the airport, Sweetie?"

"It's in the northeast quadrant of the city, and I'm lined up to come in above it," Sweetie said. "Don't worry about seeing it. In five to eight minutes there'll be light enough to see on the ground. Tropical dawn, you know."

Manning could hear the faint sounds of the wind in the Baron's rigging. The lights below increased in size with disturbing speed. The damn plane is gliding like a rock, he thought. He tried to take solace from the Frenchman's calm expression. McCarter didn't seem worried, either. Of course David was checked out to fly multiple-engine aircraft of any type up to jets. It made a difference.

"Seven thousand feet," Sweetie-Pie said. McCarter and Manning stared out to left and right. It was no longer full dark below. Indeterminate objects could be made out faintly, Manning observed. This whole damn business was making him definitely uneasy. Unpowered flight might be all right for—

"Bloody bull's eye!" McCarter exulted, pointing. Manning moved in behind him, and found himself staring down at a lightish colored rectangular space less cluttered-looking than the surrounding area. Lights burned at the four corners. Three small planes were staked out on the field, and Gary grimaced when he noted that even at their lowered height the planes looked like moths.

"So much for general aviation in Concepción," McCarter said as the field passed smoothly beneath them. "Nothing military, right, Sweetie?"

"Unless there's something in the hangars. Button it up now. The river and the abandoned field should be coming up within thirty seconds."

Gary fell silent as the glide continued. The amount of daylight had increased remarkably in just a few moments, but all he could see below now was thick, dark forest. Then there was a sudden break, a silver streak.

"The river," Sweetie-Pie said. "And the field," he added five seconds later as a lighter area appeared in the midst of forest that stretched away to seeming infinity.

"There's a plane!" McCarter exclaimed.

Gary had seen a dark blue, too, at the far end of the field. "Or a building?" he asked doubtfully.

"It's a plane," Sweetie-Pie confirmed. "Large enough to be the charter. I wouldn't have given much more than a *centavo* for your logic, McCarter, but you hit it. What now?"

The field was already out of sight. "Swing around and get us in there," McCarter ordered. "Land at the other end from the plane and roll us right up to it. When you're as close as you can get, give it a full dose from your nose spotlight. That should let Gary and me know how many are at the dance.''

The little Frenchman leaned forward and switched on the engines. The Beechcraft bucked once, then began immediately to climb. It banked to the left in a steady circle as it regained altitude. Then Sweetie-Pie held a clenched fist above his head without looking around. His other hand on the power control was like a feather.

David McCarter moved to the exit door and made ready to throw it open. He winked at Manning. ''Don't sprain an ankle when you jump out,'' he said.

14

The truck rattled and banged along the bumpy dirt road. Rafael crouched over the steering wheel trying to maintain speed while not outrunning the penetration of the truck's feeble headlights. On either side of the lights jungle stretched away into blackness.

Rafael was driving down the center of the road, a course he had decided upon after noting the sometimes horrifying drop-offs at the roadside. Where the road had been elevated in places to pass over swamps, the drop-offs were eight and ten feet.

Beside him, Yak tried to ease his cramped position in the middle of the cushionless seat. KO sat on his right. "No springs, no shocks," Yak sighed, stretching his legs. "My tailbone might not make it intact." He held a handkerchief to his face. A sixteenth-of-an-inch layer of fine grit coated the truck's interior.

"It's like traveling in your wild West must have been," KO said. "Many times I have read about riding in buckboards on dusty trails."

"We could sure use one of your bullet trains right now," Rafael growled. "I can't believe there can be transportation problems like this in the twentieth century."

"Almost the twenty-first," KO said.

"I wonder how David and Gary are doing," Yak mused.

"I'll bet on David," Rafael said. "I know he can be a moody bugger when he's sitting around, but when the bell rings I want David at my back. He has a pair of hands on him like meat hooks. They'll be there ahead of us. Way ahead of us, the way we're going. KO, you're sure we're going to be okay on communications?"

"Perfectly sure, Rafael. I changed the crystals on all the walkie-talkie sets, including David's and Gary's, before we reached Rio so we'd have a private channel here. It's just a matter of making the first contact. We should—"

He broke off as the truck rounded a curve and a light became visible. It became recognizable as a fire by the side of the road. Rafael slowed down as the flickering firelight absorbed the weak illumination afforded by the truck's headlights. Two men in uniform with carbines held across their chests stepped out from behind the fire into the center of the road.

Rafael braked to a stop. "*Hola*, sergeant," he said in Spanish as one of the men moved alongside the driver's side of the truck. The other remained in the road's center, his carbine half-slung forward. At close range, Rafael could see that both were teenagers. The one near the truck pulled himself up by the stake-board panels and peered into the body of the truck.

"Paraguayan Army," Rafael murmured to Yak.

"What are they carrying?" the soldier in the road called out in Guarani-Spanish.

"Diamonds!" the one on the side of the truck

shouted. "With a little gold and silver!" He laughed and dropped down to the road, then approached Rafael with an arrogant swagger. "Papers!" he demanded brusquely. "What are you, ditchdiggers or gravediggers?" He laughed again at his own wit.

Rafael's hands felt damp on the steering wheel. He had discussed with Yak in Asunción the possibility of picking up a gun in the back streets there. He cursed himself now that he had let Yak persuade him not to do it. With these bloody-minded kids one never knew. He hadn't shut off the truck's engine. He measured the distance to the soldier in the road. A quick flooring of the accelerator—

Yak's left hand squeezed Rafael's thigh. "If we're not going to give the papers a chance, why did we bother to obtain them?" he asked quietly.

"Yeah, you're right, Yak. Sorry." Rafael felt ashamed. For an instant there he had been close to panicking.

Yak leaned across Rafael to hand the packet of papers to the young soldier. Rafael had just noticed a place on the other side of the road where the brush seemed to have been beaten down. By the passage of vehicles? The firelight didn't extend far enough, but Rafael thought he could see—or sense—dark shapes.

"He can't read," Yak whispered to Rafael as the teenager turned the papers over in his hands.

"Maybe not, but here comes one who can," Rafael said grimly. He nodded toward the brush. Moving into firelight range from the area beyond the beaten-down, roadside jungle growth, a tall uniformed figure moved rapidly toward the truck. Rafael saw that he had lieutenant's bars pinned to his epaulets.

He took the papers away from the teenager who was trying importantly to point out the government stamps on them.

The newcomer scanned them for only a moment, then pushed the young soldier out of the way so he could speak directly to Rafael. "Who leads here?" he demanded.

"The professor, captain," Rafael said, indicating Yak.

The lieutenant examined the harsh planes and rugged cheekbones of Yak's features. "What is it that you claim to be licensed to do?" he asked.

Rafael listened to Yak's calm explanation of an archaeological dig. Out of sight, Rafael's hand rested on the truck's door handle. If anything went wrong, the very first thing that happened would be the lieutenant's receiving a faceful of door. After that, Rafael didn't care to think about it. Without even a handgun—

He could see that the lieutenant wasn't really listening to Yak's explanation. Rather, he was listening to the tone of it. He was listening for nervousness, insecurity, or other signs of guilt. But Yak was giving it a good reading, smoothly but with just a hint of impatience. A busy man extending the courtesy of an explanation to another busy man, but anxious to be on his way. Yak's academic Spanish was impressive, too.

The lieutenant held up a hand suddenly, stopping Yak in midsentence. He thrust the packet of papers through the opened window at Raphael. "Wait here," he said, then turned away and walked back in the direction from which he had come.

"What gives?" KO asked softly.

"I think Yak snowed him," Rafael replied. "But—"

Engines roared suddenly in the darkness beyond the firelight. A camouflage-painted Jeep nosed into the light through crackling brush and turned north in the same direction Mr. Fusaka's truck had been proceeding. Rafael could see four men in the Jeep. A 6x6 truck with canvas sides followed closely and turned in the same direction.

The two teenage sentries ran to the fire and kicked the lean-to of logs down into the ditch. Then they hurried to the truck and pulled themselves aboard. Rafael couldn't see how many men were inside. The young soldier who had asked for papers was waving his arm in a big arc indicating they were free to follow.

"We have an escort now?" KO asked.

"No," Rafael said. "They don't care about us. They have their own fish to fry. They made us wait because they didn't want us cluttering up the road ahead of them."

"I hope I'm wrong about what I'm thinking is the reason for their hurry," Yak said.

"I don't think you are," Rafael said. "They've got to be after the same group of guerillas that we are."

"So move it!" KO said impatiently.

Rafael shook his head. "We can't keep up with them. Why follow too closely and eat their dust? We can give it five minutes."

"It's just as well they were preoccupied with their own mission," Yak said as they watched new layers of dust and grit settle upon the hood of the truck.

"You can play that contract redoubled and vulnerable," Rafael said. He stared straight ahead through the windshield. "I apologize, guys. I came within a tick of blowing that one. We could never have outrun them. With no weapons—"

He didn't finish it.

The trio sat in silence until Rafael put the truck in motion and started up the road after the army patrol.

15

Ian Revill watched Ray Willoughby step down awk-wardly from the other dugout canoe, then splashed down into ankle-deep water from his own and waded ashore. Chama and two of his men had paddled Willoughby's canoe five miles upriver in dawn light while three more guerillas had piloted the second unsteady canoe in which Revill had been placed amidships. He hadn't known what to expect when he'd been taken from the cage in darkness and brought to the river's edge on the island before the silent journey began.

Willoughby looked exhausted, Revill thought, but he walked at a good pace along a path more felt than seen, a guerilla in front of and behind him. Revill had the same escort. The morning's heavy dew brushed off on them from all growing things until gradually they became wet from neck to ankle.

Revill estimated they had hiked two miles before the closely overgrown path widened unexpectedly in-to a clearing. In the center of the clearing, in the midst of colorfully blooming *hispangas*, was a telephone pole with drooping wires stretching away on either side. Revill stared in disbelief at this surpris-ing evidence of an otherwise nonexistent civilization.

A guerilla donned climbing spikes and swarmed up

the pole, a handset dangling from one shoulder. Just when it seemed these people were from the Stone Age, Revill thought, they produced facets of technical knowledge like this. The guerilla down-spiked his way to the ground and handed Chama the handset which Revill could see contained two headphones on a Y-cord.

He moved closer to Willoughby. "What's this in aid of?" he asked in an undertone.

"Negotiations," Willoughby replied. "It's my third trip to this place since we—since we were recaptured."

"Negotiations with Intercontinental?" Willoughby nodded. "So what the hell am I doing here?"

Willoughby shrugged. "I'd guess in case a question came up about where or when your plane could fly out of here."

"You're that far along in the negotiations?"

Willoughby's attempt at a smile was a wintry grimace. "No. Not at all. Chama just must have felt you should be here."

Revill had been looking up at the telephone line again where the guerilla had made his cut-in. "How do they keep their calls from being traced?"

"They have a surprising technical facility," Willoughby said wearily. "Among the guerilla branches." He nodded toward the telephone pole. "Chama contacts the Bolivian guerillas who held us originally. They contact Intercontinental head-quarters—I never knew how—and we're somehow patched through. I don't know if even telephone technicians can trace such a call."

"Where are they getting all this know-how?" Revill asked.

"I assume—" Willoughby broke off when he saw Chama beckoning to him urgently. He went and sat down beside the guerilla leader, putting on the second headphone. Chama was wearing the other one.

"Tell him what I told you to tell him," Revill heard Chama growl in Spanish.

Willoughby listened in silence for a moment before clearing his throat. "Yes, this is Ray Willoughby," he said before listening again. "I anticipated you'd tell me again that Mr. Carling isn't available for negotiations, Winston, so I have a message for you. Tell Mr. Carling that if he isn't available to negotiate during the next call, the call will be placed instead to the *New York Times*. The group here would rather have money, but they'll settle for publicity."

There was another gap in the conversation. "Shut up, Winston!" Willoughby broke in suddenly. "Don't try to give me that corporate responsibility bullshit! I'm trying to keep my ass together here! Do you understand that?"

He listened again. "Right, and let me give you a personal message also. If it's the company's intention to let us dangle here, as far as I'm personally concerned someone had better speak to the guerilla leader here and order me killed. Because if I somehow make it out of here with no help from you, my first stop will be Intercontinental headquarters where I will personally guarantee to reshape a few Intercontinental asses! Tell Mr. Carling that, Winston!"

He snatched off the headphone and thrust it at Chama. The latter, frowning, spoke forcefully into his own. "Same time tomorrow morning, Raoul," he said in Spanish. "No, I think we've bled this pig all it's going to permit. Have your statement ready for the newspaper."

The young guerilla climbed the pole again and retrieved his tap-in. The group marched back to the river and the canoes. Ian Revill might even have enjoyed the floating trip back to the island had it not been for the river odor and the ferment in his mind. It had never occurred to him that the Intercontinental people might not be eager for prompt renegotiations.

It was still early enough when they returned to the huts that there was no sign of activity. Revill was led back to his cage. He stood to one side as a guerilla unlocked it. The man shouted something unintelligible and rushed inside the cage. The other men crowded around the cage door.

Peering beyond them, Revill could see that the loosely replaced earth where the iron bars had been dug out was scooped to one side. Two of the bars had been bent outward enough to permit a thin body to wriggle out.

Terry Conrad had escaped.

16

McCarter looked over his shoulder at Manning as the Beechcraft touched down and bounced lightly. "Keep one alive!" he shouted, then turned and forced the door open when he felt the pull of the plane's brakes. He gauged their forward speed with an expert's eye, then launched himself into a dive that ended up in a shoulder roll.

He scrambled to his feet in time to see Gary Manning hit the ground fifteen yards behind him. With a huge swing of his arm, McCarter indicated they should separate and form a pincers movement. Manning went to the right, McCarter to the left.

Ahead of them, the Beechcraft continued onward until it seemed as if it would plow into the Nord rescue plane. The spotlight in its nose came on, pinpointing a dark figure that sprang up from the ground. The man staggered backward, trying with an arm to shield his eyes from the glare focused upon him while the dark bulk of the Beechcraft seemingly pursued him. The man's mouth was open in a scream rendered soundless by the noise of the Beechcraft's engines.

The watchdog guerilla turned to run. "Don't let him get to the river!" McCarter yelled. Unsure whether he could be heard above the engine sound, he redoubled his own sprint effort. The guerilla, veering toward Manning, made it off the hacked-out runway into the shelter of the brush.

Manning, whom McCarter firmly believed could run for two days and a half but was devoid of foot speed, pounded along behind the man, the recently acquired P-15 in his right hand. His woodsman's ways enabled him to glide through obstructions where the guerilla crashed through them. He was gaining, but slowly.

McCarter, with more natural speed and coming from an angle, closed the gap more rapidly. Still, he could see the glint of the river before his oversized right hand clamped down upon the running man's shoulder. The man's upper body remained in place for an instant while his legs continued running. Then David jerked him backward so forcefully that the first part of him to hit the ground was the back of his neck.

Manning was there immediately to lend an unnecessary hand. "Drag him—back from—the river-bank!" McCarter panted. Together they did so. Manning, still breathing easily, patted the guerilla down expertly as the man lay inert.

Gary looked up at McCarter. "Only a knife. Did they leave him to guard the plane without a gun?"

"I have a hunch we'll find it at the charter aircraft where he dropped it when he took off," David said. "Sweetie's spotlight probably spooked this character into thinking his Indian gods were after him."

"What now?" Manning asked.

"Check the river bank and see if he had any kind of water transportation."

Gary at once jogged down to the river's edge. He explored the bank for a hundred yards in each direction, but found nothing. "Not a thing," he reported upon his return.

"That means whatever they're using is on the other side of the river and this type here had to wait to be relieved. That makes two things we need to know from him—when the next guard change takes place, and where his buddies are."

The guerilla was erect now, standing between them. "I don't know if he can understand you, but he's putting his game face on," Manning warned. He was looking at the man's stolid features and flinty-looking expression.

"When I put on *my* game face, his will turn to shit," McCarter answered. "Or at least it better had for his sake." He turned to the guerilla. "When you relieved?" he asked in halting Spanish.

The guerilla stared at him stonily.

17

Sergeant Pedro Caceres set down his early morning coffee while he stared incredulously at the jungle-camouflaged Jeep and canvas-sided truck that pulled to a stop in front of his chicken-wired military compound on the outskirts of Concepción. Men piled out of the Jeep and truck and stretched lengthily, stamping their feet in the manner of soldiers who had been riding for a long time.

Caceres straightened up from his heel-sitting position outside the one-room office that was one of two buildings in the thirty by thirty-foot compound. The other was a sun-shriveled barracks. Heedless of the dust stirred up by the newcomers' arrival, Caceres ran to the chicken-wire gate to open it. "Lieutenant Alsogaray!" he said joyfully to the tall man with lieutenant's bars on his epaulets who had been the first to step down from the Jeep.

Caceres started to thrust out his hand, then caught himself. He snapped off a salute, realizing in the instant he did so that he was barefoot and wearing only uniform trousers. His lean shoulders and arms were laced with white-ridged scars, souvenirs of numerous knife fights.

Lt. Alsogaray returned the salute, then shook his head slowly as his gaze took in the sergeant's unmilitary appearance and the general air of neglect in the paper-strewn, cluttered compound. "Is this how you maintain order, sergeant?" he asked sharply. "Why haven't your men policed this area this morning?"

Caceres shifted his glance to the barracks.

"You mean they're still in there? Turn them out!"

"Inspection!" Caceres blared in a buglelike tone. "Inspection! All out!"

For ten seconds nothing happened. Then a tousled man with sleep-smeared eyes stumbled from the barracks. He was wearing only ragged underwear, but he was carrying an AK-47 assault rifle in one hand and trying to clamp on his head a shiny, new, dark green, steel helmet with the other. He drew himself up to attention.

One by one three more men joined the first. Each was in a similar state of undress. Behind them came two flat, round-faced, single-garmented young girls who would have lined up beside the men had not Caceres's ferocious glare sent them fluttering around the corner of the barracks out of sight.

"Sergeant, you're a disgrace to the army!" Alsogaray barked.

"Yes, sir," Caceres agreed meekly.

"Have these men shape themselves up and shape this place up! Then come into the office!"

"Yes, sir," Caceres repeated. He rasped out the necessary orders hurriedly, then was first into the barracks to make himself presentable. He emerged five minutes later, pistol strapped to his web-belt, an efficient-looking field soldier, albeit one rated not nearly so high on a garrison standard.

Out in the street the fully equipped men from Jeep and truck milled aimlessly. Caceres estimated there were nearly twenty of them. Something was really going on to find them here with Lt. Alsogaray. The lieutenant was one of General Stroessner's trouble-shooters in the field.

The lieutenant had appropriated Caceres's chair, the only one in the boxlike office. Caceres came to attention before the three-legged, propped-up desk. Alsogaray waved a dismissing hand, then extended the same hand across the desk. The two men shook hands warmly.

"Sergeancy does not become you, Pedro," the lieutenant said mildly.

"Ahh, Lieutenant!" Caceres said reproachfully. "How could you let me make such a mistake?"

"I couldn't stand in the way of your ambition," Alsogaray said, smiling. "You were determined to become a sergeant."

"But in the field!" Caceres protested. "And with you, as before! Not this—" he swept an arm around him, "—not this miserable housekeeping!"

"The field might be arranged," Alsogaray said.

"I'd light a candle to the Virgin!" Caceres said eagerly. "Every day for a year! Why do you say it might be arranged? What's going on?"

"You have guerillas in the area, Pedro."

"Of course," Caceres said. "Always. It's in my reports."

"I have read your reports. There is not much detail."

Caceres smiled. "I had a former superior officer who told me that if there was enough detail in a report to enable headquarters to act without consulting me directly, then there was too much detail to do my career any good.''

"Now why does that sound familiar to me?" Alsogaray was smiling, too, but then he turned serious. "It is time for details."

"You mean—" Caceres broke off abruptly. "The planes!" he said quietly. "That's why you're here. The guerillas have done something with the planes." But then he frowned. "There has been no talk in the town. Always there is talk when they are up to something."

"Someone is enforcing more discipline. Where are the guerillas, Pedro?"

"I can show you their island. I have been out there twice and swum around it. I have marked what I saw on a map."

"You've been out to the island recently?"

"Not since the planes," Caceres said regretfully. "I should have realized—"

"Let's see your map."

Caceres moved around behind the desk and removed a ragged-looking map from a side drawer. He opened the map and flattened it out on the table in front of the lieutenant. He placed a finger upon the largest island shown in the river off Concepción. "The little crosses are what I've seen of guerilla emplacements and outposts."

"Excellent, Pedro, excellent." Alsogaray was making quick sketch marks upon the map with a silver pencil. "You can find boats to take us out there?"

"Easily. But I have a favor to ask."

The lieutenant leaned back in his chair, his expression watchful. "You envision a successful field operation? You're going to ask for a battlefield promotion? You should know that General Stroessner makes up his own mind about those matters."

"If we're successful," Caceres said doggedly, "I'd like to become your corporal again."

Alsogaray laughed. "A battlefield *de*motion? Agreed. One three-day drunk after our field exercise, following ensuing disciplinary action, you will be my corporal again." He bent down over the map. "Headquarters says there are six hostages in the guerillas' hands. The general wants them recovered, if possible, but primarily he wants the guerillas taken and brought to Asunción."

Caceres looked dubious. "These hostages—" he began.

"I know," the lieutenant cut him off. "It will be a fire fight, and they will have to take their chances with the rest of us. I want us on the island with an hour of daylight left, Pedro. That's today. And I want no chance of this developing into trench warfare. I want to roll right over them. What do you suggest?"

The planning went on for another hour.

18

The excited exclamations of the guerillas around Revill brought Chama on the run. "What is it? What is it?" he kept asking as he pushed his way through people. None of his men wanted to put it into words. Chama shoved people aside until he was far enough inside the cage to see the bent-out bars which mutely proclaimed Terry Conrad's escape.

Chama literally howled with apoplectic rage. "After him! After him!" he screamed. "Don't let him get off the island! Who was the guard responsible for this? *Who was the guard?* I'll feed him his fried ears!"

Again no one answered. Chama's burly figure seemed to swell inside his khakis. His face turned almost purple. His eyes hollowed. He grabbed the nearest man by the arm. "Answer me!" he bellowed. "Who permitted this to happen?"

"I don't know," the man said quickly. He was obviously terrified. "I was—I was just up-river with you!"

Chama growled something unintelligible, then wheeled to leave the cage. He almost ran into Ian Revill who stood hemmed in by the milling bodies. "You!" Chama rasped in a tone that made the word an epithet. "You were part of this!" He snatched a carbine from the closest guerilla and slammed its butt into Revill's chest.

For an instant Revill felt only the power of the blow that sent him staggering backward. Then an excruciating pain surged upward from the point of impact. It filled his throat, filled his mouth, filled his nostrils. He doubled up slowly and fell to his knees, then rolled over on his side. He was fully conscious but he couldn't breathe.

He expected Chama's boots to come thudding into his exposed ribs, but he couldn't draw his legs up to afford himself any kind of protection. The lightning bolt of pain had passed onward from his nose to his ears. He could even feel it behind his eyes. A quick surge of nausea racked him, but his constricted throat refused passage.

He had been surrounded by legs when he fell. Struggling for breath that wasn't available, he became aware that the legs were gone. Chama was gone. He didn't have time to think about it because another onset of nausea forced a thin trickle up his flaming throat from which it dribbled from his mouth. Turn your head more, he urged himself. Do you want to choke to death on your own vomit?

Hands seized his arms roughly and jerked him upright. He almost screamed. His legs doubled up involuntarily until he was supported entirely by the hard-gripping hands. He didn't think he could ever straighten out again. He would have pleaded to be set down on the ground again if he could have made his throat work.

The hands carried him from the hut's dimness into the searing sunshine outside. They dropped him roughly in the shade of the huge quebracho tree which marked the jungle's closest encroachment. Blackness rolled up on him like a switched-off TV screen but then receded. He remained on his side, motionless, afraid to move because the pain might increase.

Someone knelt down beside him, and he flinched. Every internal fiber seemed to contract upon itself so great was his fear of another brutalizing blow. One eye was in the dirt. He kept the other one closed.

"How are you doing?"

The English words were a shock. Revill opened his upper eye slightly. It was Ray Willoughby who was kneeling beside him. "What—you doing here?" he whispered with tremendous effort.

"Chama realized he let himself get carried away. He needs you to fly the plane. What happened?"

"Gun butt—chest." A five-mile run couldn't have called for more effort than that necessary to get out the words.

"Can you turn onto your back?"

Revill felt hands upon himself. He resisted, but the hands insisted and slowly moved him from his side to his back. He heard himself gasp twice, but at least he didn't cry out.

"Let me unbutton your shirt and we'll have a look," Willoughby said. Revill closed his eyes again while his shirt was unbuttoned. Willoughby took Revill's limp hand and placed it gently on Revill's chest. He could feel a hard lump already forming at the bottom edge of his breastbone.

"Can't tell if anything's broken," Willoughby continued. "But as usual it could have been worse.

Two inches lower and he'd definitely have ruined a few vital parts."

Revill wet his dry lips with the tip of his tongue. "What—about Conrad?"

"They don't seem to have him yet. They're out thrashing around in the jungle. That state of affairs probably won't continue much longer. There's no place for him to go."

"Gutsy," Revill whispered. "What he—did. I was digging—with him, but I'd—never have gone." The speech renewed the fire in his upper body, and he subsided.

"I'll get you some water, which is about all I can do. The best thing for you is rest, anyway."

Ian Revill stared upward into the branches of the quebracho tree and waited for the water.

19

David McCarter removed a knife from a forearm sheath and wiped off nonexistent dust on his thigh. The knife was double bladed and had a rough bone handle. The blade was four and a half inches long. The knife was beautifully balanced, and it looked wickedly efficient.

Gary Manning saw the guerilla's eyes flick toward the knife, and then away. The man had recovered from his initial fright and the alarmingly sudden appearance of the Beechcraft, but McCarter definitely had his attention now. Despite his game-faced stoic appearance, it wasn't hard to perceive that the man wished he were anywhere else.

"Talk," McCarter said to the man in his halting Spanish. "Where is your camp?"

The man made no reply.

McCarter took a step closer and jabbed at the guerilla's face with the knife. The man's arms came up instinctively and crossed in front of his threatened face while he stumbled backward. McCarter pulled his punch, hooked off the jab, and landed a solid stab to the guerilla's belly.

Gary Manning's stomach lurched before he realized that McCarter had turned the knife blade under in his hand. It had been his bare knuckles that had landed. The guerilla didn't recognize it that quickly.

He screamed hoarsely while he collapsed upon his heels, a hand clasped over his presumably knifed stomach. With his other hand he pulled up his shirt to feel for the wound. His agonized expression turned blank when he was unable to find it.

McCarter showed him the knife. "Let's try it again," he said.

The man's brown features crumpled like wet aspirin. *"No más, no más, no más!"* he pleaded. His eyes glistened with fear. Voluble Spanish poured from him in a flood. McCarter had to hold up a hand to slow down the flow so he could understand it.

"Upriver," he translated for Gary. "Four kilometers. The large island."

"Ask him if the hostages are there," Manning suggested.

The man nodded a vigorous affirmative when McCarter asked the question in his primitive Spanish.

"And you wanted to know when his relief was due," Gary reminded.

"Yeah, that's right." McCarter put the question. "Sundown," he said. "Gives us time to set up here. Well, that puts a period to the usefulness of this type."

"I'll tie him up," Gary said hastily. McCarter started to say something, then changed his mind. Manning advanced upon the kneeling man and ripped his shirt from his back. He tore it up into strips, then motioned for the guerilla to cross his wrists behind his back. The man complied eagerly.

Gary marched him to the charter plane after tying him up, pushed him to the ground under the plane's wing, removed his belt, and lashed his ankles together tightly. McCarter had followed to observe. The

knife had disappeared back into his forearm holster.
When Gary straightened up from his task, McCarter
was looking speculatively at the Beechcraft, which
Sweetie-Pie had parked under the much larger wing of
the charter.

"Why haven't we seen Sweetie?" McCarter asked
himself aloud. He moved to the Baron, opened its
door, and swung himself up and through it.
"Asleep," he reported to Manning over his shoulder.
"Charging up his batteries for his return flight. He
thinks." He scratched his jawline, the rasp of his two-
day beard plainly heard. "I'll just take a couple of
plugs from each of Sweetie's engines so we have a vote
about when he leaves."

"What would you have done if the guerilla hadn't
talked?" Gary asked curiously when David had removed the plugs and stowed them carefully in a
pocket.

"Followed through," McCarter said with a shrug.
"Like you'd have done."

Gary wondered if he would have been able to do it
himself.

"Not with the knife, necessarily," McCarter said as
though reading his mind. "I wasn't actually planning
to use the knife myself. It gets late early with that kind
of deal, and we needed him alive until he'd talked. It's
rarely a problem. Everyone talks when the right button is pushed. There aren't nearly as many hard men
around as the would-be hard men would like to think.
There's only a man in every four or five hundred who
can really tough it out. And invariably he's a bloody
freak."

"A freak?"

"Yeah. Of some kind. Religious, maybe. Or political. Whatever. So this guy would have talked eventually. He just made it easy on himself."

"But if you weren't going to use the knife, and if he hadn't talked—"

McCarter grinned. His light blue eyes were jovial looking. "I had a little exercise in mind for him. Learned it in Jordan with the SAS. Strip him down, see? Then a bucket of water over his balls. Then several bootfuls of this—" he kicked at the loose, sandy earth "—to stick to the wet parts. This alluvial silt's more abrasive than carborundum, y' know. Well, maybe seven percent less. Y' get him onto his feet and run him, with a knife jab in the ass every time he slows down."

He grinned again. "Clears a man's mind something wonderful, in addition to taking all the skin off his privates. Perspiration helps, and he supplies it. Thing of it is, he knows he can stop running if he starts talking. Like I said, there's few who don't."

"What happens to the few who don't?" Gary asked quietly.

"In that particular case? Oh, permanent damage. Absolutely. Erodes the sac. You gotta have balls to tough it out...and then you don't have 'em after all!" He looked up at the sun. "Hop aboard the plane and get our walkie-talkies from our bags, will you, Gary? I'd like to think we'll be hearing from Yak and the others before too long."

Gary went to the plane to get the walkie-talkies.

He couldn't get out of his mind the grim picture David McCarter had so blithely described.

20

Dawn had come to the potholed dirt road to Concepción along which Mr. Fusaka's truck had been bumping for what seemed an eternity. Rafael still had to pay close attention to his driving. They had fallen so far behind the Paraguayan army patrol that even in the weak daylight they could see no dust clouds marking its passage.

Yak broke a long silence. "Imagine what this must be like when it rains!" he said. He was fiddling with a walkie-talkie in his hand over which he had been calling Blue Fox Center at irregular intervals.

"They shut down the road," Rafael said, intent upon his driving. The road seemed even more narrow along this section. Upon the infrequent occasions they passed a car or a truck coming the other way, it was necessary to slow down to ten miles an hour to assure safe clearance.

"I could use a pit stop," KO spoke up from his corner of Mr. Fusaka's truck cab.

"Yeah, so could I, now that you mention it," Rafael agreed. He waited till the truck was on a section of road fractionally wider, then pulled in as tightly as he could manage to the trees on the right-hand side. He climbed down from behind the wheel into the roadway and stretched lengthily. Yak followed him, walkie-talkie in hand. KO had already stepped down into the ditch on his side of the truck.

"We've *got* to be getting close to Concepción," Yak said to Rafael. "I'm concerned we haven't raised David and Gary on this thing." He gestured with the walkie-talkie.

"I've been watching the odometer, too," Rafael admitted. "It does seem like we've been getting our kidneys pounded forever. What bothers me, though, is whether there's a point to all this. I lost about twenty-five or thirty points worth of confidence when that army patrol pulled into the picture."

"It's not good," Yak agreed. "We're hypersensitive on the subject, of course, but it really does seem that a hard-driving night patrol like that in country like this could have only the same target in mind. What else of any consequence could be going on in this desolate area?"

KO climbed up from the ditch and was listening to them. He pointed to the walkie-talkie in Yak's hand. "Walk up the road a bit and try it," he suggested. "Away from the truck's bulk. Despite their five-watt power, these things are only line-of-sight operational, and with all the jungle mass around us the transmission distance is bound to be limited."

"Not a bad idea," Yak said. He walked up the road in the direction they had been driving. Rafael descended into the opposite ditch. Yak pulled out his walkie-talkie's antenna and depressed the microphone button. "Blue Fox One calling Blue Fox Center, over," he said as he had been saying a dozen times before during the past hour. "Blue Fox One calling Blue Fox Center, over."

There was silence for an instant, and then a faint burst of unintelligible sound emerged from the unit in Yak's hand. "Hey!" Rafael exclaimed delightedly. He scrambled up the bank into the road again. "It's got to be them!"

KO trotted up the road to Yak, holding out his hand. "Let me try, please?" he said. Yak handed over the walkie-talkie. KO placed himself where Yak had been standing and began a monotonous repetition of Blue Fox One calls, each time moving his feet slightly so he was covering ninety degrees of a circle. Twice he drew similar unintelligible sounds from the unit and paused, but then continued.

And then suddenly Gary Manning's flat Canadian accent sounded so loudly in their ears in the jungle silence around them it seemed he could be heard all the way back to Asunción. KO reached instinctively for the volume control, but then withheld his hand.

"—repeat, come in, Blue Fox One," Gary's voice said. "This is Blue Fox Center. Repeat, come in, Blue Fox One."

"Blue Fox Center, this is Blue Fox One," KO said into his microphone. While speaking, he drew a line with his boot in the dusty road in the direction he was facing, then glanced downward at the miniature compass attached to his belt. "We are receiving you on an extremely narrow band clearance, otherwise very poorly. How do you read me?"

"Weakly, Blue Fox One," the unit said. "Hold on."

David McCarter's voice spoke up almost immediately in his clipped British accent. "Blue Fox One, where are you?"

"In a truck on the road to Concepción, an unknown distance south of it."

There was a slight pause. KO could picture David and Gary discussing the situation. "We have no knowledge of that road, Blue Fox One," McCarter's voice resumed. "Except that sky geography indicates it won't help you to reach us. We suggest you mark the compass direction on which we're coming through to you most clearly—" Rafael pointed down at KO's bootmark in the dirt, then circled a thumb and forefinger "—then stash the truck and walk through to the river. It can't be more than two miles, and it could be half that. We'll be able to pick up your signal better on the riverbank, and we'll talk you gents in."

KO glanced toward Yak and Rafael. Both nodded at once. "Affirmative, Blue Fox Center," KO said. "You have a contract. We're on our way. Out."

He slid the antenna down and returned the walkie-talkie to Yak. Rafael was already looking thoughtfully at the roadside, which was a seemingly impenetrable mass of second-growth trees, vines, and brush. "This is gonna call for machetes, guys," he said. "And perspiration." He climbed up into the body of the truck.

He handed down their bags first, then two machetes and a long-handled axe. He rooted around for a moment and passed down a shovel. While he and KO walked along the roadside, looking for an area where the least cutting needed to be done, Yak opened all three traveling bags, removed from his own three nylon, dark green backpacks, and began to assemble a two-day supply of civilized necessities upon each.

KO and Rafael spent an hour hacking out a space into which Rafael could back the truck. They were sweat stained by the time they accomplished it. Rafael removed the distributor cap and hid it in the truck body beneath the rest of Mr. Fusaka's landscaping equipment. He carried an old tarpaulin back down to the ground with him and snugged it around the truck's engine.

He and KO picked up brush they'd cut and stacked it strategically in front of the truck's blunt nose and its windshield. They moved out into the center of the road to inspect their handiwork. "Whaddya think, pal?" Rafael asked.

"Only the white stubs of the newly cut area show up," KO said. "Otherwise someone would have to stop right in front of it."

"One good rain shower will take care of the brush," Rafael said confidently. "You can stand around after a rain in this country and watch stuff jump right up out of the ground."

Yak had finished packing all three backpacks—the final item in his own being two of his prosthetic arms—and joined them. "I hope we never need the truck again," he said.

"But there it is, if we do," Rafael said. He looked at the dark green forest. "Okay, guys? We'll still need the machetes, KO. Lay out the course and strike up the band."

KO checked his compass, each man slipped into the arm straps of his nylon backpack, and they edged their way into the mini-jungle confronting them.

Neither Rafael nor KO offered to take Yak's pack, an offer which they knew would be indignantly refused.

21

David McCarter reclipped his walkie-talkie to his belt and turned to stare appraisingly through the trees toward the river. "It'll probably take them three or four hours to get here," he said. "Meantime we'd better be unpacking the bloody crates."

"We're going to set up right here?" Gary Manning asked.

"We'll set up two posts at the edge of the airstrip that command a converging field of fire focused upon the path coming up here from the river. We know we're going to have at least one caller at sundown, and it could be more."

He led the way toward the Beechcraft with Gary following. When McCarter opened up the cargo-area door, Manning moved in front of him and began muscling the crates to the loose earth. Two of the crates had painted on them in red letters No Hammers or Axes. The other two were unmarked.

McCarter grinned when he saw the marked crates. "Sweetie-Pie takes care of his customers. Those will be the ones with the ammo and the plastique, flares, grenades, and mortar rounds." He bent down to look at the marked crates more closely. "Screwed together, not nailed like the others," he said. "I saw a large screwdriver in the same locker with Sweetie's private war chest.''

He climbed up into the Baron while Gary walked the crates apart to give himself some working room. He guessed that it was only 10:00 A.M. by the height of the sun, but it was already beating down mercilessly. Gary paused to remove his shirt. His upper-body development was remarkable with bulging biceps and pectorals.

David emerged from the Baron with an eighteen-inch screwdriver, a ball-peen hammer, and two chisels. He handed the hammer and chisels to Gary, then started unscrewing the bolted crates. Gary inserted a chisel between a nailed slat and the crate proper and knocked it loose with the hammer.

"We want the Uzis?" he asked.

"Correct," David replied. "With Yak arriving shortly to look over our shoulders, I want to set this ambush up properly." Gary raised an inquiring eyebrow. "I got off on the wrong foot with Yak when we first met," McCarter continued.

"I remember," Gary said, smiling.

"So I want to show him I'm not the slob I appeared to be then. What are you doing next month?" David asked in a quick change of subject.

"Next month? I'll be back in Toronto diagramming terrorist tactics to unbelieving industrialists. Why?"

"Money. Any chance of your slipping over to London for two or three days?"

"Why?" Gary asked again.

"Money," McCarter repeated. "There's a marathon in Kent I'd like to enter you in. And, you know, get a few pounds down. Actually, more than a few."

"I'm not that good, David."

"You'd be good enough for this," McCarter persisted. "I've checked the field."

"Street marathon or countryside?"

"Countryside."

"That's better, but it could still be iffy. If the course record is two hours, eighteen minutes, say, I'd probably run it five to eight minutes slower. If there was a world-class runner in the field, I'd be a half mile or more behind him."

"There isn't," David said. "And the price would be right, because you're the most unlikely looking marathoner the world has ever seen. The boys in the pubs would hold me upside down to make sure they'd emptied my pockets."

"Well, we can talk it over later."

"It would be a beautiful touch," David said.

They had been working while they were talking. Gary removed two Uzis from the second of the unmarked crates and carried them to the edge of the airstrip. McCarter followed him and indicated where he wanted the submachine guns stationed, about forty feet apart. McCarter crashed down to the river's edge, stamping down brush and small bushes as he cleared a line of fire. He reversed himself and came back to the other machine-gun post, doing the same thing en route.

He paused to wipe his forehead with his sleeve. "Clear out a back line, too," he told Gary, suiting the action to the words at the machine-gun position where he was standing. "We've got to be able to cover the airstrip and keep whoever from reaching the planes. But we won't set up near the planes because we don't want to draw fire toward them. Tonight we'll—"

· "Blue Fox One to Blue Fox Center," Yak's voice said clearly from the walkie-talkie at McCarter's belt.

"Blue Fox Center raht heer," McCarter replied in a burlesque of a southern accent.

"We're at the river, Georgia Brown."

"Recite the British Football League standings, over."

"Recite the *what*?"

"Or the Articles of Incorporation for the Israeli government, if they have any," McCarter continued, grinning. "Or the second verse of the bloody *Marseillaise*. Keep talking. I want to get a fix on your voice position, over."

Yak began to recite "Horatio at the Bridge." McCarter kept pivoting with the unit in his hand until he was facing in the direction from which Yak's voice was loudest. "Okay, done and done, Blue Fox One," he said finally. "You're south of us. Come north up the riverbank and we'll stage a joyous reunion. Aren't you glad that floods clear out the banks periodically and the jungle doesn't grow right down to the water?"

"We're glad. Any word of our target area, over?"

"We've all but got a fence around them, over," McCarter said cheerfully.

"Excellent. We'll be right along, Blue Fox Center. Out."

"Now that's what I like to hear," McCarter said to Gary, returning the walkie-talkie to his belt. "Action coming up. Speaking of which, let's cuddle with the

Uzis and hike south to meet our brethren. It's not bloody likely they'll run into enemy action, but I doubt they have any arms, and wouldn't we feel like proper idiots if they did?''

They started down toward the river, each with a Uzi cradled in his left arm.

22

Rafael Encizo knelt in mud up to his waist while he sawed vigorously underwater just above the root of a tough-fibered hollow reed. Above him on the river-bank, Keio Ohara was making up two waterproof packages from a torn-up poncho that could be tied to the tops of their heads and fastened under their chins. The principal weight in each package would consist of a Beretta Model 951 9mm Luger.

Rafael stood up and tossed two reeds up on the bank. He sloshed himself up and down in the water rapidly to rid himself of most of the clinging mud, then climbed up on the bank himself. "When I trim mouthpieces on these babies," he said, "they'll make perfect snorkels."

KO was staring across the river at the low, green-mounded bulk of an island. "That's got to be it, you think?" he asked.

"Got to be," Rafael answered. "It's the largest and it's four kilometers upriver from the airstrip, just like David said."

David McCarter's "joyous reunion" had quickly turned into a council of war. A renewed sense of urgency had been instilled in David and Gary by Yak's news of the army patrol in the area. They had returned to the airstrip to find Sweetie-Pie awakened from sleep and bemusedly inspecting· David's machine-gun posts enfilading the riverbank.

The Frenchman had been introduced to the rest of the group and had sat cross-legged with them while he listened silently as the evening's activities were planned. "Reconnaissance first," Rafael had declared. "KO and I will swim out to the island and check out the guerillas' numbers and setup there, as well as what will be necessary to get the hostages off the island afterward."

"And if everything checks out on the reconnaissance, let's hit the bloody island at dawn," McCarter proposed.

There were no negative votes. Yak looked across the circle at Sweetie-Pie. "When do you feel you have to leave?" he asked in French.

"Midnight," the Frenchman replied. "But I'll fly downriver after takeoff so the engine sound won't alert the guerillas to the fact there's activity in their vicinity."

"It shouldn't be a problem, anyway," McCarter chimed in. "The jungle acts as nature's muffler in blotting up sound, except for the stretches straight up and down the river where sound is funneled."

So Rafael and KO had left the airstrip to hike upriver to the island. Just before leaving, Rafael had watched Gary Manning giving water to the sullen-faced, tied-up guerilla, whom Rafael hadn't noticed before. He had looked inquiringly at David McCarter, who had returned his look blandly and said nothing.

Rafael turned now for another look at the island that was clearly illuminated by the setting sun. "Do we strip?" KO asked while he fastened the poncho package on top of Rafael's head.

"We do *not* strip," Rafael returned emphatically. "There are leeches in this water that don't like people. Leave your boots only." He was eyeing the current with an expert's eye. "About five knots, I'd say. Which is a hell of a lot more to push against than most people realize. We'll have to swim in an arc."

He tested the firmness of the package tied to his head, then picked up the other one and placed it on KO's head. He had just begun to fasten it when KO gripped his arm suddenly. "What—" Rafael began.

KO's hand pressure increased, and Rafael fell silent.

Wordlessly, KO pointed upriver where sunlight glinted sharply from the dark green helmets of uniformed men in rowboats, which were drifting down upon the island. Rafael and KO both dropped flat upon the riverbank instinctively.

"Damn, damn, damn!" Rafael murmured softly, raising his head just enough to keep the armada in view. "This makes it a whole damn new ball game!"

23

Twilight was settling down upon the river at the airstrip. Long shadows stretched away to seeming infinity. David and Gary were at their posts with their Uzis crooked in their arms, staring at the darkening water. It was not many minutes since sunset, the time when the exchange of guards should be taking place according to the guerilla from whom David had forced the information.

They both saw it at the same instant, a rowboat swept along by the current, close to the bank. A man sat in the bow, a man sat amidships, rowing, and a man sat in the stern with a rifle or carbine across his knees.

David and Gary surged up to their knees as though wound by the same spring. The rower stroked strongly with his right oar, and the boat darted in toward the bank. It shoved its nose up on a mud flat briefly before the current carried it out into the stream again. During the interval the man in the bow stepped down and began to ascend the bank.

The oarsman held the boat in place ten feet out in the river with a slight feathering of his oars. They were waiting for the man relieved from guard duty to come down to the river for his trip back to the guerilla island.

Capture the first man when he gets to the airstrip, Gary thought, and a second will follow eventually to express his displeasure at the delay. The third man would be a different problem. It would take a really stupid guerilla to climb the incline after the disappearance of two predecessors who didn't respond to calls.

But the new guard stopped before he had come a third of the way. He peered suspiciously up the rise toward the airstrip. Did he think he saw something, Gary wondered? There was nothing to see. He and David had made sure of that.

But there was no doubt he thought he saw something. The man turned with a hoarse shout and began to run back toward the boat. David and Gary rose simultaneously. Animal instinct, Gary thought as he touched off his Uzi a tick behind the sound of David's. McCarter's Uzi-burst picked the man up and flung him to the right. Gary's pinned him in midair for an instant before he fell back to the left, a bundle of bloody rags.

The men in the boat gaped openmouthed, the oarsman over his shoulder. He dug hard with his oars to get the boat started away from the bank. The man with the carbine stood up in wobbly fashion as the oarsman's jerky movement spun the boat in the water. He raised his carbine and tried to aim it.

The dimples from the bullets of Gary's Uzi in its renewed burst walked across the river to the boat and peppered its stern, half landing in wood, half in flesh. The man with the carbine, crouched against the boat's bucking movements, straightened up convulsively, sagged backward, and disappeared into the dark-looking water. The released carbine fell into the boat.

The rower stood up, abandoning his oars. He dived for the carbine, but David's prolonged rat-a-tat-tat raised little puffs of dust from his uniform as the burst hemstitched him from shoulderblade to shoulderblade. The man collapsed, half in and half out of the boat, before his weight slowly overturned it.

The man's body plunged into the river.

The boat floated away, upside down in the current.

24

The first scattered sounds of automatic weapons fire brought Ian Revill's head up from the tuft of pampa grass upon which it had been resting. His first thought was that the guerillas had finally found Terry Conrad after searching for him in vain all day while Chama grew more and more furious. But the firing, coming from the north end of the island, increased in volume and frequency until Revill realized suddenly that the guerillas were under attack.

He had moved very little since being dumped on his back by the guerillas where he was after being dragged out of the cage. Twice he had tried sitting up, only to be overwhelmed again by the same searing flame that surged up through his throat from his breast where the carbine butt had been slammed into it by Chama. He was additionally alarmed by the fact that his legs wouldn't work properly. He had spoken to no one except Ray Willoughby, who had twice brought him water again during the long afternoon. Both times the conversation had consisted of a brief "How are you?" and a muttered "Not too bad."

A prolonged machine-gun burst and the excited shouts of surprised guerillas seeking cover in the central hut made Revill realize his own exposed position at the edge of the clearing. He could still see the hut clearly, although the light was fading. He forced himself to turn his upper body over onto his belly, fighting off waves of pain that alternated with mini-blackouts.

His legs refused to turn over completely, remaining crossed at the ankles. Ignoring that disturbing fact, Revill pulled himself along on hands and elbows until he was deeper in the jungle edge and twenty feet removed from where he had been. He could hear the ragged return fire of the guerillas in the hut, which only seemed to bring down upon them an increased fusillade.

Yells, shouts, and cries of pain mingled with the smell of cordite wafted toward Revill by the evening's river breeze. He could hear the occasional ringing clang of a bullet ricocheting from a bar of the cages, and he thought pityingly of the hostages inside them, almost totally exposed, but hugging the ground.

A guerilla ran from the hut and tried to reach the trees to the south. The automatic weapons fire, much closer, cut him down. Revill could see an occasional muzzle blast in the deepening twilight as the attacking force advanced steadily. Another man broke and ran, while Revill could hear Chama's huge bellow of rage. The second man fell sprawling to the earth, and Revill couldn't decide if the bullet that had felled him had come from the attackers or from the hut itself.

The question was answered almost immediately. Chama himself charged from the hut, machine gun across his chest, bandoliers glinting. He ran toward Revill's position while Revill instinctively sought to burrow himself into the soft ground. Chama stopped suddenly, digging in his heels. He raised the machine gun waist high and fired a creeping barrage that obliterated the pampa grass and small bushes where Revill had been previously stretched out on the ground.

Crouching low, Chama then wheeled and ran toward the woods. He had been hit; one leg was dragging. A bullet turned him sideways, but he staggered onward. At the edge of the trees he was hit again and the machine gun flew from his hands, but he limped into the trees amidst the gathering darkness.

The sounds from within the hut had changed in character. There were shouts of surrender now, and pleas for mercy. A powerful voice raised itself from the northern woods confronting the hut. "Cease firing and throw your weapons out!" it blared in Guarani-Spanish, then repeated it twice more.

The firing slowed, then stopped.

An uneasy silence settled down upon the clearing.

"Come out one at a time with your hands on top of your heads!" the powerful voice bugled.

Revill could see uniformed, green-helmeted men, weapons at the ready, shielding themselves behind trees at the edge of the clearing while they waited.

One by one guerillas emerged from the hut, weaponless, hands clasped on top of their heads. Revill counted seven before the exodus stopped. Seven? It didn't seem like enough. But then there would undoubtedly be men inside who couldn't walk out, including men who would never walk again. He wondered anxiously how the hostages had made out.

The soldiers advanced into the clearing, encircling the guerillas. "Clear the hut, sergeant!" a tall lieutenant said briskly. "Then move our wounded out first. And send a guard into the jungle after escapees."

In response to a sharply barked command, the guerillas sat on the ground, surrounded by soldiers. The lean-looking sergeant took two men with him and entered the hut cautiously. His voice rose almost at once. "Lt. Alsogaray!" he called loudly.

"Yes, Caceres?"

"Come and take a look at this!"

Revill watched while the lieutenant strode to the hut. He rubbed the back of his neck, which ached from holding it up while he watched. And the pain in his chest and throat was enormous in his new position. He wondered uneasily if anything had happened to his lungs.

Two of the men were plunging sharp-ended torches into the ground, which they lit to cope with the gathering darkness. The lieutenant emerged from the hut, saying something over his shoulder that Revill couldn't hear to the sergeant who followed him. "— get on with it," the lieutenant was saying when he faced forward again. "If we move it out of here, we can deliver these animals tomorrow and not have to spend the next day's holiday out in the bush."

A squad left the clearing, heading into the jungle toward the south end of the island. Sergeant Caceres designated four more men to move the army's wounded. "Put them aboard the guerillas' barge," he said.

The light from the torches fell mostly on the side of the clearing away from Revill. There was a shout from the jungle, and two soldiers appeared with a roughly handled guerilla between them. They spun him down contemptuously into the circle and went back into the woods again. The newly captured man looked around sheepishly at his friends.

Sergeant Caceres had just started to say something

to Lieutenant Alsogaray when a high-pitched voice spoke from so close to Revill that it startled him. "Hi, there!" the voice said. "I'm an American!"

Terry Conrad walked from the brush out into the clearing with his hands up in the air.

Ian Revill felt as though he was watching a slow-motion movie. The swing of two AK-47s toward Conrad. A third that was a tick slower. All three bloomed at the muzzles simultaneously, and Terry Conrad's slight body jumped upward, pitched sideways and sprawled motionless upon the ground.

There was an instant's silence after the sound of the execution cleared itself from the ears. Sergeant Pedro Caceres exploded, "No order to fire was given!" he roared.

"But the guerillas, sergeant," one of his men said in an apologetic tone. "One cannot wait."

"Idiot, did you ever see a white guerilla in a white shirt?" Caceres growled. He crossed the clearing to bend down over the body, then turned away. He looked toward the lieutenant and spread his palms wide. Both looked toward the jungle as another shout was raised.

Revill noted dully that the man being led in by four guerillas was Chama. Five minutes previously he would have sworn the sight would have made him the happiest man in the world. Chama walked without assistance, even wounded as he was. Not that much would have been offered, Revill thought. Human life obviously meant no more to the army than it did to the guerillas.

Chama eased himself down to his knees, then sat. There was no particular expression on his swarthy face that Revill could recognize. Even his eyes seemed smaller. The guerilla leader placed himself a little apart from his men. There was nothing in his dress to indicate any insignia of leadership, and his machine gun—the previous badge of his authority— was gone; but Revill saw the lieutenant looking at Chama speculatively.

Chama's men were marched to the barge two and three at a time. Their hands were tied behind their backs before they left the clearing. The movement took almost an hour during which the torches burned low. Caceres and two of his men went into the hut then and one by one brought out the hostages.

There were only four of them.

Two men and two women.

Harold Dobbins and Kenneth Holt. Muriel Miller and Jennifer Gossage.

Revill stared at them. They stood like four human shells. Blank expressions on empty faces. It was as if they were more dead than alive.

Terry Conrad was dead, of course. And then Revill realized Ray Willoughby was missing. . . .

Two by two the hostages were moved to the barge and the tiny engines were started. A single torch flared erratically in the silence of the clearing. For a time Revill could hear the diminishing sound of the tiny outboard motors as the barge worked its way upstream.

Then the silence was complete.

25

Rafael and KO stood amidst the trees on the west bank and ruefully watched the feeble running lights of the guerillas' barge disappear upriver. "Do you think there's any point in going out to the island now?" KO asked quietly.

"Damned if I know," Rafael replied moodily. He stared across at the island, a darker bulk against the increasing blackness of the night. "How could we get a lousy break like this? We've blown the deal. No guerillas, no hostages. Although I really don't see what we could have done differently."

"What happens to the hostages now, Rafael?"

The Cuban shrugged. "I suppose they go to Asunción where the dictator produces them triumphantly out of the goodness of his heart. I'm damned sure all he really wanted was the guerillas captured so he could hang them from plaza lamp posts and show the world the old lion isn't losing his teeth." He was still staring toward the island. "Maybe we should go out there anyway, KO. Yak is going to want to know all the details about this, and so is Mack Bolan. God alone knows who it is he's going to have to tell the story."

"Fine with me," KO said.

They began to finish off their nearly completed

preparations. Rafael knelt beside his pack on the bank and produced two pairs of goggles, one of which he handed to KO. He also brought out two waterproof penlights, which they clipped to their belts. "'Course, there's another way of lookin' at what happened," Rafael said as they climbed down the bank into the lukewarm water, carrying their reeds. "If we'd been an hour earlier, we'd probably have fallen into the army's bag, too. Okay, let's go."

He struck out upriver in a long arc aimed at propelling them against the current and eventually depositing them at the north end of the island. Rafael throttled down his own water progress to match that of KO's, who was a powerful but relatively untrained swimmer.

Rafael was both powerful and trained. It seemed a long time back to his training days. He had practiced water infiltration and underwater demolition with Brigade 2506 at Base Trax, Guatemala, prior to the Bay of Pigs invasion during which he had been captured. These days he had deliberately forced from his mind all memory of the ghastly days in Principe Prison.

He watched the island carefully during the swim. There was no real reason for the army to leave a rearguard that he could see, but it never hurt to be careful. Certainly there was no sound except the soft lapping of the water in his ears. The stars, which earlier had seemed like pale fireflies, now loomed large and seemingly only a hundred yards overhead.

He almost ran into the shoreline before he saw it ahead. He glided in against the bank, motioning for KO to do the same. Rafael pulled himself along the bank, using roots and other underwater growth. KO followed him with a bit more involuntary splashing than Rafael felt comfortable with, even though he anticipated no trouble.

They came to a wide, low place in the bank, seemingly scoured out of the shoreline growth. Rafael put his feet down and encountered yielding mud. He waited until KO was alongside him. "This was where the barge was moored," he muttered. "We might as well go ashore here."

They waded in cautiously. Where the bank began, Rafael removed his snorkel reed from his belt and jammed it down into the mud. Again, KO followed suit. Rafael removed his head package and unwrapped it until he could fit into his hand the Beretta 9mm Luger. Then he climbed the bank with KO right behind him.

The single lighted torch left by the army patrol was flickering badly, but its light disclosed the perimeter of the clearing. Rafael could see huts off to one side. He could also see the twinkle of expended brass cartridge shells upon the ground. It had been a short but fierce fire fight.

A body on the edge of the clearing nearest the huts caught his eyes. He went over to it and dispassionately examined the ragged uniform. A guerilla body, as he was sure it would be. The army patrol would have removed any casualties of their own.

KO hissed at him from across the clearing, and Rafael went to join him. KO was on one knee beside a white-shirted, white-faced, young-looking, doubled-up man who had been cut almost in two by automatic weapons fire. KO looked inquiringly at

Rafael who had hunkered down on his heels for a closer look.

"I don't get it," Rafael said slowly. "That's got to be one of the hostages. Nobody should have wanted to kill him, guerillas or army. Unless one of the guerillas lost his head when he realized his own ship was goin' down."

"Let's hope he's not the one we were supposed to bring back to Washington," KO said.

"Yeah. Not that we're likely to bring anyone back, the way it looks right now." Rafael shook his head when he considered the money and effort expended to no avail.

"I'm English," a hoarse voice said from what seemed yards away. "Don't shoot."

Rafael and KO flew apart violently as though electrically shocked. They ended up flat on their stomachs on opposite sides of the body, Berettas trained upon the spot from which the voice had come.

"I'm the copilot of the hostage plane," the voice said. "The patrol overlooked me."

"Looks like we overlooked you, too," Rafael said when he had renewed the saliva in his mouth. "Walk out of the brush, copilot."

"I can't walk."

"So crawl, man. Crawl."

There were a few seconds of silence followed by a shuffling, crackling sound. A man's head appeared, thrust forward above braced elbows. Rafael lined up on the head carefully, but KO, whose angle of vision permitted him to see the immobile, dragging lower body, stood up and went nearer. "It's okay, Rafael," he said. He reached down and straightened out the legs that were still crossed at the ankle.

Rafael lowered his Beretta and also stood up. He couldn't think of anything to say. "Where are you shot?" he got out finally.

"Not—shot." The voice was a husked whisper, racked with pain. "Gun butt—in chest. Motor muscles inoperative. Turn—me over, please?"

They got him onto his back. At first his breath came in quick, rasping sobs, but it gradually quieted. They could see his face in the starlight.

"You flew the hostage plane?" KO asked.

"Copilot," the man said again. "Name's Revill. Ian Revill. Forced—down. Pilot killed—by Chama."

"Chama?"

"Guerilla—leader." Rafael tried to raise his head. "Afraid there's—one more hostage inside—the nearer hut."

"I'll take a look," KO said immediately. He walked to the hut, removing his penlight from his belt. Inside, its thin beam circled the entire area quickly, then returned to linger upon a pile of guerilla bodies in one corner. He counted five. The beam moved onward and picked out the cages. KO stared. Then he stepped forward and rapidly beamed the light around the interior of each cage. He lingered at the last one before he backed away and went outside.

"—mad dog," Revill was husking to Rafael who was again kneeling beside him. "He killed—Charles Gargan, my friend. He ruined—the woman's—mouth. He tried—"

"Mouth? What woman?" Rafael interrupted.

Revill explained haltingly about Muriel. "He tried

to—kill me, too, and—would have succeeded—except I had—crawled away from where—his men had dropped me." Revill looked up at KO standing silently beside Rafael. "And he killed—Ray Willoughby, too—didn't he?"

"If Ray Willoughby is his name. There's a dead man in a cage inside," KO explained to Rafael. "Shot in the head at close range. Visible powder burns."

"A mad dog," Revill repeated. "Willoughby was the senior Intercontinental hostage."

"Listen," Rafael said, as though forcibly rousing himself, "what we got to do is get our asses out've here, like right now. KO, help me carry him down to the barge mooring." He addressed Revill again. "Sorry, but this is going to hurt a bit."

"I'll—manage. What are you—planning to do? Neither—of you looks equipped—to live off the country."

"We'll take you back to the airstrip. There's a few more of us there."

"Airstrip?" Revill opened eyes that had been closed. "The airstrip—where my plane is?"

"The same."

"Have you—a boat?"

"No boat, but it'll be a piece of cake," Rafael said confidently. "C'mon, KO."

They carried Ian Revill to the barge mooring.

Once again he had difficulty with his breathing, but he made no sound.

Rafael went into the strip of jungle separating the barge mooring from the clearing, carrying his knife. He cut large hollow reeds resembling bamboo and lianas, then stripped off huge plant leaves called elephant's ear.

He carried armfuls of each to the mooring and used the vines to lash the reeds together into a rectangle into which he interwove the plant leaves. He stood the resulting raft up on end and punched its center but was unable to put his fist through it.

"Piece of cake," he repeated, smiling.

They loaded Ian Revill aboard Rafael's raft and carried the raft knee-deep into the river where they set it down in the water while Rafael checked it for leakage. He added a few more strategic leaves and indicated to KO that they were ready to go.

Ian Revill felt the movement as they waded out shoulder-deep with the raft. He opened his eyes again and tried to focus upon the island which showed up only as a menacing black mound. "Hellhole," Ian Revill muttered.

KO placed himself at the front and Rafael at the rear, and together they angled the raft across the current while they floated downriver toward the airstrip.

26

They sat in a circle at the airstrip: Yak, Gary, David, Rafael, KO and Sweetie-Pie. Ian Revill lay on the raft, which Rafael and KO had carried him on from the river. Yak had examined Revill and regretfully concluded there wasn't much they could do for him except keep him as comfortable as possible until they returned to civilization.

David had suggested a fire and when there had been no objection, the unspoken consensus being that the time for hidden maneuvering had passed, he had laboriously axed chunks of wood from a wind-downed, iron-hard quebracho tree. The small fire burned with a clear, smokeless flame. They sat at a respectable distance. They had no need of its heat, given the high humidity of the mild night.

A silence had fallen after the conclusion of Rafael's detailed report upon events at the island. Yak in his Sorbonne French had concisely translated for Sweetie-Pie who sat beside him. The pair had struck up an amiable relationship almost upon introduction. David McCarter was sprawled upon his back, hands locked behind his head. Gary Manning stared into the fire's dancing flames. In the north woods he had sat around more campfires than the rest of them put together.

Yak sighed as he looked around the circle at the subdued group. "I suggest we brainstorm it," he said in a tone he tried to make brisk. "To find out if there is any opportunity open to us."

"There isn't," David said at once. "The dice just stopped rolling, and they're reading craps."

KO had been pitching tiny pebbles into the fire. "Where will the four hostages and the guerillas be taken now?" he asked of no one in particular.

"Jail?" Gary hazarded.

"Army headquarters," Rafael said in the same breath.

There was another silence while they considered it. "I doubt jail," Yak said at last. "It doesn't seem to me the general would want his ordinary criminals exposed to the ideas of politicals like the guerillas."

"And the bloody army keeps a lower profile than that," David said. "They might stand the guerillas up against the wall as traitors, but I think General Stroessner would prefer to turn them over to the courts to emphasize once again his abhorrence of communism." He grinned at Rafael. "I've never understood, Pescado, why Stroessner is regarded with as much distaste in Washington as in Moscow."

"Because of the goddam bleeding-heart liberals in the State Department!" Rafael said hotly. "The same ones who never gave us the support—" he didn't finish it.

"Politicals are not taken either to the civil jail or army headquarters," Ian Revill said unexpectedly. All eyes turned toward him. He was speaking with less difficulty but his voice was still very hoarse. "The dictator does not wish either his ordinary criminals or his army units exposed to the insurrectionist poison of politicals.''

"So where do they go?" KO asked.

"There is a place two blocks from Government Palace, on a side street. It is run by an elite group. It has no official name, but all over the country it is known as The Holding Place. There is an entrance from the street, but it is all underground. I'm told it's three tiers deep.''

"It sounds like dungeons," Gary observed.

"It's probably a fair description," Revill said. "Very few return to society from it, and those who do have nothing to say about it.''

"You think the hostages will be taken there as well?" Yak asked with doubt evident in his tone of voice. "Why would the general pass up an opportunity to improve his public relations?"

"Because the general has tunnel vision in regard to communists. They will be in the forefront of his mind. Besides, I *know* the guerillas will be taken there, and as the lieutenant said on the island, with a holiday on the following day it's unlikely any of the general's aides will interest himself in the hostages until that's over.''

"It's a risk," David said. "And *if* the hostages are taken there, *then* we walk in and demand that they be handed over to us?" He sounded disgusted.

"What would it take to walk in there?" Yak asked.

"Uniforms," KO said. He looked at Revill. "Army uniforms?"

"Or police," Revill said. "The police are paramilitary.''

"That's all right," Rafael argued, "but we'd need a story, too. Some sort of a con job."

"Just brainstorming," Gary said. He was sitting with his hands locked around his knees while he stared dreamily into the clear flames. "If we had uniforms, we could be delivering a captured guerilla there."

"A captured guerilla?" Two or three voices said it in unison.

Gary jerked a thumb over his shoulder in the direction of the tied-up guerilla, the original plane guard, who was sleeping under the wing of the charter plane. "Him."

David started to laugh. "What a bloody joke if that would get us inside!" he said. He looked around at the group. "I can guarantee that if it hadn't been for Gary we wouldn't have had a guerilla to consider delivering."

"I wondered about that," Rafael admitted.

"And when we deliver him," Gary continued, unheeding, "then we also tell the commandment we're there to move the hostages elsewhere."

There was another silence while they all considered it, Yak translating for Sweetie-Pie.

"Maybe we're looking at the big end of the funnel first," Rafael said finally. "Maybe we can get inside there, okay. But what about getting out of the country afterward?"

"It wouldn't hurt to consider it," KO said dryly.

"We have the Nord," Revill said.

"The Nord?"

"The charter plane."

"Ahh, I see," Yak said. "But—you'll forgive me—we don't have the Nord's pilot."

Gary was looking at McCarter. "David? Can't you fly that thing?"

"Sure," McCarter replied. "After a couple of days to check it out. Unless Revill here cares to sit in my lap while I try to get it out of this airstrip."

"I don't really believe that sitting in your lap should be necessary," Revill returned. "Will the copilot's seat do?"

McCarter stared. "You're not—you can't—" he stumbled over his words and started over again. "Physically you're not able to do it."

"My feeling is that I'll be no worse off in the copilot's seat than anywhere else," Revill said.

Rafael was smiling. "You sound to me like a guy mad at someone," he said.

Revill's return smile was wintry. "I object to having my life so drastically rearranged with no input from me. I hold no brief for anyone in this damned country, guerillas or government." He looked at McCarter again. "What does your certificate qualify for?"

"Anything up to jets," David said. "Mostly military, though." Listening, Gary thought the answer was delivered with something less than his friend's usual bravado.

"There's another factor," Yak pointed out. "Isn't this a marked plane? Won't it be known as the hostage plane wherever it flies? Or, more particularly, wherever it lands?"

"Yeah, there is that," Rafael said thoughtfully. "How do we get around the hole in that doughnut?"

"We don't know that any information was released publicly in Paraguay," Revill said. "If not, it's been retained at the highest levels. My feeling is that if my plane landed at Presidente General Stroessner Aeropuerto at the freight terminal side of the field, say, supposedly to pick up a cargo, not too much attention would be paid to it, especially with what's bound to be skeleton crews on hand due to this National Independence holiday."

"We might even be able to turn it around," Gary suggested. "Suppose the plane lands and is challenged, for any reason. We could be there to openly move the hostages out after General Stroessner's heroic recovery of them."

"Not bad," Revill said. "That's not bad at all. It's bold enough that no minor flunky should even dream of challenging it. And the lack of papers would be because this is a special hush-hush project of the dictator's."

"It's thin," David objected.

"But plausible," KO said.

There was another pause, which was broken unexpectedly by Sweetie-Pie.

"I've flown several times into the freight terminal at Presidente General Stroessner Aeropuerto to deliver or pick up patients," he said in French. Only KO and Rafael looked at him blankly, unable to understand. "When there, I call an ambulance which delivers or collects my patients. If your group was aboard an ambulance, who would question their presence anywhere in the city?"

"Sweetie—" David McCarter said jubilantly, jumping to his feet "—I think you've found the bloody missing link. Weapons could move unseen in an ambulance, too."

Yak explained the little Frenchman's remarks to KO and Rafael. Both men nodded. Yak turned to the Frenchman. "Are you volunteering to make such a flight?"

"I'm sure your organization would reimburse me for my expenses," Sweetie-Pie said.

Yak smiled. "I'm sure it would."

"The ambulance could take us to The Holding Place," Rafael visualized it. "Then it could return the hostages to Revill's plane. The rest of us—" he shrugged "—well, we'd just have to commandeer something."

"We'd have to take over the ambulance driver," KO said.

"A very, very minor detail," David assured him. He moved around the circle of men to Sweetie-Pie, a bland smile on his face, and held out to the French-man the plugs he had removed from the Beechcraft's engines. "Here you are, Sweetie. I thought I'd clean these up for you."

"Thanks, but I replaced them with spares after I ran my usual post-flight checkup and found the plugs missing," Sweetie-Pie returned with no particular emphasis.

McCarter laughed.

KO was speaking to Yak. "How do we know the main object of the mission hasn't already been blown, Yak? With two of the six hostages dead already, the horse may be gone from the barn. Doesn't it make a difference?"

Yak glanced significantly at Ian Revill.

Rafael, who had been listening, spoke up. "Yeah, he's not supposed to know about the number one priority, Yak, but he does. He heard us talking about the same thing on the island before we knew he was laying there in the weeds.'' He hesitated for an instant. ''Speaking for myself, after seeing the guerilla gorillas operate, I'd favor going an extra mile to free the rest. Besides, that's the mission.''

''I'll second that motion,'' David McCarter chimed in. ''They are particularly unlovely people.''

''How are we going to get uniforms?'' KO asked.

''Not peaceably,'' McCarter grinned.

''How would it be if we rolled up to The Holding Place in the ambulance and went in all dressed in whites?'' Gary proposed.

''It *could* work, but—'' Yak began.

''I can't see it,'' Rafael interrupted. ''In uniform, we'd walk in there with our weapons looking like part of the uniforms. In whites, carrying weapons, we'd look like virgins at an orgy. I think it has to be uniforms.''

''But on the street, whites might be a plus,'' Yak said. ''Who looks twice at doctors or medics? Maybe a combination of uniforms and whites?''

Rafael shook his head. ''In uniforms, we'd have the extra benefit of looking the way we'd be expected to look.''

''One thing that could help is the holiday itself,'' Revill put in. ''There's a big parade, which draws upon almost all police and army units in the capital. Jails never close, of course, but staff is likely to be at a minimum.''

''Hurray for minimums,'' David said.

''Uniforms,'' KO said again.

No one spoke.

"Okay, except for uniforms do we have a plan?" Yak asked. It was discussed by all with rising enthusiasm. Yak looked around the circle where heads nodded one by one. "Then I suggest we sleep on it for now and tackle it again in the morning," Yak said. "And everyone focus his dreams upon how we're going to acquire the necessary uniforms."

The meeting broke up.

Rafael and KO carried Ian Revill on his raft away from the fire and placed him near the planes. "Anything we can do?" KO asked.

"Yak gave me some pills," Revill said. "I don't feel too bad. My legs are hurting now. For a while I was afraid they were never going to hurt again."

Rafael and KO wrapped themselves in ponchos and joined the rest in badly needed sleep.

27

An hour after dawn David and Gary carried Ian
Revill to the Nord. He was still on the raft, which
made a convenient stretcher. The three-step descending ladder was under the wing of the plane where it
had been sitting since the hostages climbed down it
after the force-down. Gary put it in position,
mounted it and opened the passenger door.

Together he and David raised Revill from the raft
as gently as they could. They carried him up the ladder and into the cabin of the Nord, then along the
aisle to the cockpit door. The cramped space there
and inside the cockpit wouldn't permit the bulk of
three men's bodies. McCarter, with his bull-like
strength, carried Revill inside alone, kicked the
copilot's chair sideways on its swivel, and settled
Revill in the chair. The Nord copilot's face was
white, his eyes were closed and he was breathing
heavily.

McCarter turned Revill's chair forward and locked
it in position. He seated himself in the pilot's seat and
began studying the instrument panel while he waited
for Revill to recover from the necessary rough han-
dling. Gary sat down on the cockpit floor with his
back against a wall. Despite the night's comparative
coolness, the accumulated heat inside the closed-up

plane was stifling. All of them were perspiring freely.

Revill opened his eyes and began to lead David through the Nord's preflight checklist. David placed a finger upon each instrument or navigational aid as it was mentioned. Revill's voice was wispy at first but gradually attained renewed resonance. His deep-sunken eyes indicated the extent of the pain he was experiencing, but he made no mention of it.

McCarter looked from time to time through the pilot's side window along the length of the earthen airstrip. "This baby has bounce getting off the ground?" he asked finally. "I've seen croquet fields with more straightaway than this airstrip."

"Not quite," Revill said with an attempt at a smile. "And the plane does have bounce. You'll have no problem."

"A piece of cake, as Rafael would say," Gary said from his position on the floor.

David turned to glare at him. Then he laughed, but not very robustly. "You'd better hope it's a piece of cake," he said grimly before turning back to his lesson.

They stayed with it for ninety minutes before Ian Revill's responses to David's questions became more and more monosyllabic. Gary punched McCarter in the leg to indicate that enough was enough, and they carried Revill off the plane. They all breathed in gratefully the cooler air outside, ignoring the malarial night mist still rising from the river. "We can do it again this afternoon?" David asked hopefully after Ian Revill had been restored to his raft-stretcher.

"Surely," Revill said.

His eyes were closed again, but he made his voice strong.

Yak convened a meeting at midmorning. They met at the machine gun emplacements on the rise overlooking the river. No one expected trouble, because no one knew of their presence, but still Yak had the emplacements manned. The river afforded the only convenient way to get at them, and Yak had no intention of permitting themselves to be walked in upon unhindered.

He had designated Rafael and KO as the gunners. They spoke no French, and it was Sweetie-Pie who would have the floor during the meeting. Yak and Revill spoke fluent French, Gary his Montreal brand and David a sixth-form academic variety. Yak would convey the sense of the meeting afterward to Rafael and KO.

He handed a notepad and pencil to Sweetie-Pie. "Draw us a map of the freight cargo buildings at Presidente General Stroessner Aeropuerto," he said. "With particular attention to street exits."

Sweetie-Pie looked distrustfully at notepad and pencil. He smoothed a square on the ground and began to draw with a twig, talking swiftly as he did so. His speech was so laden with street argot and slang that even Yak and Revill had to listen closely. Twice the little Frenchman stopped to confer with Revill in asides having to do with airport distances and directions. Yak quietly transferred to his notepad the drawing Sweetie-Pie was shaping on the ground.

"There must be soldiers at this cargo depot, aren't

there?" Yak asked following one of these consultations.

"Oh, sure."

"Do you know where their post is?"

Sweetie-Pie considered, staring down at his drawing. "All I can tell you is I see most of them in this area," he said, placing the twig upon a smaller building than others he had drawn. Yak made an *X* upon his notepad.

"If it helps at all," Revill contributed, "the leaders of the army patrol which attacked the guerillas were a Lieutenant Alsogaray and a Sergeant Caceres."

"It may indeed help," Yak said, writing it down. "I think this thing is beginning to shape up." There was a note of satisfaction in his voice. He looked around at the group. "I'll bring Rafael and KO up-to-date now, and we'll all get together again later."

KO listened silently to Yak's explanation, nodding that he understood. Flat on his belly, his eyes never left the river his machine gun covered. Yak walked across the intervening distance to Rafael's spot.

"I have an assignment for you, Sergeant Caceres," Yak said in a formal tone.

Rafael gaped at him.

Yak explained swiftly the significance of the name and a possible use for it. Rafael's eyes began to shine. "It'll work, Yak, it'll work," he said emphatically. "And if it doesn't, we'll just blow the bastards away."

"It shouldn't come to that, if we're to be successful," Yak said. He walked back to where the group was breaking up. "Gary, David—relieve

Rafael and KO." He would have moved on but Ian Revill stopped him with a raised finger. "Yes?" Yak asked.

"On the island," Revill said, "your men were concerned because your group's interest was in rescuing one among the hostages in particular, and they felt with two already dead their chance had been reduced by a third. If it will stiffen your resolve—if it needs stiffening, that is—I can tell you I think the one you seek is in The Holding Place."

"Why do you say that?"

"Because I've had time to think about it, and because of the natures of the deceased. An agent with a special concern could not have been Willoughby. He was far too senior a multinational officer to risk his career. Young Terry Conrad, while a bit more possible, seemed to me too flighty, too unstable, to be part of an organization of the type that commissioned your group. Their psychologists would have screened him out. So I think your man—or woman—is still available to you."

He paused. "I think we can eliminate another, the woman Muriel." He explained Muriel's ordeal to Yak as he had before to Rafael and KO. "Such folly in calling attention to herself in such a situation is hardly the work of a professional."

"I hope you're correct in your feeling," Yak said. That left Harold Dobbins, Ken Holt and Jennifer Gossage.

He walked to a tree, sat down in its shade, turned to a fresh page in his notebook, and then printed, "NATIONAL INDEPENDENCE DAY, 8:00 A.M.,

PRESIDENTE GENERAL STROESSNER
AEROPUERTO.''

He leaned back, crossed his legs, and stared unsee-
ingly across the river. Fleeting images of other places,
other enemies, other wars, crossed his vision. Then a
solitary figure, in black, standing in a huge green
meadow, intruded. And grew larger until Yak could
see who it was. The message was clear. . . .

28

The Nord had been moved away from its nosed-in position against the woods at the end of the airstrip. It sat now with its rapidly spinning propellers pointed down the limited runway. Dust and fine particles of sandy dirt flew backward from its prop-wash.

Yak, wearing a beret from his bag cocked at a jaunty angle, stood surrounded by Rafael, KO, Gary, and David. Ian Revill was already strapped into the copilot's seat of the Nord. Sweetie-Pie was aboard the Beechcraft Baron, running through his preflight checklist.

"The first step is the most critical," Yak said to the others. "If it fails, we're still close to the planes. But once past the first hurdle, I really believe we can knock this thing over on its back."

"Piece of cake," Rafael said confidently.

David McCarter pursed his lips, shook his head, but said nothing. Gary smiled as his friend restrained his usual pessimistic comments. KO's inscrutable gaze was fixed upon Yak. He reached under his loosely hanging shirt bloused over his trousers, pulled out a Smith & Wesson Model 59 9mm automatic and handed it to Yak.

Yak accepted it. He held it aloft in his left hand almost in the manner of a starter ready to send off a field of runners. "Good luck," he said. The others wheeled almost in unison and walked toward the Nord. Although not in cadence, it seemed more like a march than a walk. Yak watched them go. He would fly south to Asunción with Sweetie-Pie in the Beechcraft.

McCarter supervised the inner locking of the cabin door before he walked up the aisle to the cockpit. He belted himself into the pilot's seat while he glanced across at Ian Revill. "This is bloody well it," he said to his fellow Briton. "Now?"

"Now," Revill said after a final look at the instruments.

McCarter dropped his hands upon the controls and kicked the brake loose after pushing the throttle in. The Nord rumbled slowly away from the far end of the airstrip, then began to accelerate. The speed increased, but not rapidly enough to suit McCarter. His lips tightened.

But then the rumbling lessened, then ceased. David looked again toward Revill, who was watching the line of approaching trees. Revill nodded, and McCarter pulled back smoothly on the yoke. The Nord lifted gracefully, clearing the trees by a considerable margin. McCarter released a pent-up breath.

"Well done," Revill said quietly.

"Well done!" McCarter echoed. "I'm afraid to check to see if I need a change of underwear."

He banked the Nord, growing more confident by the moment, and flew back over the strip. He waggled the plane's wings triumphantly when he saw the tiny figure of Yak still standing there. He thought he saw Yak wave in return, but he couldn't be sure.

He headed them south, lining up the compass reading Revill had previously given him.

Back in the cabin, the passengers released their seat belts. Neither Gary, Rafael, nor KO said anything, but all looked happier than they had five minutes before. Iron-nerved upon the ground, they were less so in the air.

An hour earlier, Rafael and KO had transferred the opened and unopened crates of weapons from the Beechcraft to the Nord. Gary had crate planks strewn all over the rear of the cabin, and he returned immediately to emptying crates and stacking their contents upon the unused passenger seats.

The Uzis he gave a seat to themselves. He sat down again and began to load 9mm bullets into the twenty-five-round magazine clips. He loaded each Uzi and then attached a second magazine to the first in a ninety-degree L-clip that doubled the submachine gun's potential firepower. The extra weight under the barrel contributed to limiting the recoil action, which was one of the Uzi's more comforting characteristics. Most comforting of all was the fact that, despite the most prolonged use, the Uzi rarely jammed.

When he had the Uzis loaded to capacity, Manning continued to load clips, which he placed in pouches with straps that enabled them to be slung over one shoulder and under the opposite arm. Gary moved across the aisle then and carefully filled one of Yak's dark green backpacks with grenades. That pack he set aside for himself.

He looked around the cabin to see if there might be something he had overlooked, but he was unable to find anything. They were as ready as they were ever going to be. He sat down in the front of the plane with the others. Each man already had in his belt the handgun of his choice, along with as much extra ammunition as he had chosen to carry.

No one had anything to say. Each was quietly preparing himself mentally for the upcoming action he knew confronted the group.

Ian Revill had already been on the radio to the Asunción tower. The tower's attitude to the announced approach of Nord XN-9691 had been so casual that Revill could only assume Asunción's skies were relatively clear of other air traffic.

"Nord XN-9691 to Asunción tower," he said again. "What is the freight terminal runway number?"

"Number six, Nord XN-9691," the tower replied after a seven- or eight-second delay. "Make your approach from east to west across the river."

David banked the plane toward the east while he reached for the intercom. "Belt up, men," he sent his voice back to the group in the cabin. "We land in five minutes."

Revill pointed out to McCarter the individual runway well removed from the runway complex of the airport proper. "Any sign of Sweetie-Pie?" David asked as he completed lining up his approach run.

Revill turned his head, which with his hands was all he could move the way they had him strapped into his copilot's seat. He caught a glimpse of a sun-dazzled white object in the sky slightly to their rear and a bit higher. "Right on schedule," he reported. He eyed through the windshield their rate of descent. "You're doing fine, David."

Beads of perspiration adorned McCarter's brow as he nursed the plane down. At the last moment the runway came up with a rush. David grunted as they hit too hard and the Nord bounced high but then settled down at once in a series of shorter bounces. They rolled to a stop as David touched the brake with the freight warehouses and loading docks directly ahead of them.

Ian Revill, although white around the lips from the initial impact of the landing, saluted McCarter with a thumbs-up gesture.

In the cabin, Rafael had already unbelted himself and crowded up against the window, which permitted him to see past the tail surface of the plane. Into his line of vision rolled the Beechcraft Baron, which stopped a hundred yards away.

"They're down," he announced.

They settled down then to waiting for Yak to appear.

29

Yak paused in the open door of the Beechcraft Baron while he removed from a pocket the coins he had acquired at Los Miradores Hotel. He handed them to Sweetie-Pie to use to make his phone call to the ambulance service.

The Frenchman stepped down to the tarmac and Yak followed him. A wooden guard post at the end of an Anchor fence contained two soldiers who looked out at them indifferently. Sweetie-Pie went off to a phone booth.

Yak had time to stroll around the plane three times in an apparent leg-stretching exercise before one of the soldiers leisurely detached himself from the guard post and moved across the soft-feeling macadam. He had a carbine slung across his back, and he kept looking at Yak's beret as he approached. He had a hard-looking face and a drooping mustache.

"I have a man in the plane there with a broken leg," Yak said before the soldier could speak. He pointed toward the Nord. 'I want you to tell me how to move him."

"I'll get my sergeant," the soldier said after puzzling for an instant over Yak's classroom Spanish.

"It will be quicker if you come with me," Yak said, taking the soldier's elbow lightly and walking him away from the Baron toward the Nord. The man hesitated, but then allowed himself to be persuaded. Yak saw the cabin door of the Nord open as they neared it and the three-step platform was lowered into place in front of it.

"Have you been in the army long?" Yak asked over his shoulder as he started up the steps.

"Seven years," the man replied. He was a step behind Yak who moved inside and then quickly to one side. The soldier was bent forward slightly as he paused to look around as much of the cabin interior as he could see from the second step.

His feet never touched the top step. David Mc-Carter and Rafael Encizo stood on either side of the open cabin door. They each seized the soldier under an armpit and propelled him inside with tremendous force. The man's head hit the opposite wall with a sickening crunch.

"Don't let blood get on the uniform!" McCarter barked. He was already closing the door again, leaving the platform in place outside. Rafael was stripping off his own clothing while KO and Gary removed the uniform from the body of the soldier. Yak stood to one side with an eye on his watch while the transfer was accomplished.

"Shit!" Rafael exclaimed while trying to button the soldier's shirt upon himself. He could only fasten two buttons. "Look at this!"

"It's plain to see that the Paraguayan Army Quartermaster Corps doesn't need to concern itself with nineteen-inch necks and forty-eight-inch chests," Gary observed. "David will have the same problem. Do what you can with it."

The trousers, loose-fitting upon the soldier, experienced stretched seams before Rafael managed to wriggle into them. He took one look at the size of the man's boots, then retained his own. "Ready, Yak?"

"Ready."

Rafael picked up the soldier's carbine, then followed Yak down the steps of the platform after Gary reopened the cabin door. They marched with Yak closer to the guard outpost, partially screening Rafael. They met Sweetie-Pie walking across the tarmac, coming from the depot.

"The ambulance will be here in twenty minutes," the Frenchman said to Yak. "The name of the guard commandant is Gonzalez. I'll gas up now."

He continued onward toward the Beechcraft.

"Captain Gonzalez's office?" Yak asked when they reached the depot. They walked along the corridor pointed out to them. The commandant's office was littered with crushed cigarette stubs on both sides of the counter that divided the room. Captain Gonzalez himself was seated at a desk reading a magazine, and even from that distance Yak could see that it was a girlie magazine.

He raised his voice. "Captain Gonzalez?" he called. A nameplate on the desk eliminated guessing.

The man at the desk looked up and examined them incuriously. He looked at Yak's beret, fleetingly at Rafael, then back at the beret again. Finally he rose to his feet and ambled toward the counter. He was a man of short stature with a pencil-thin mustache, and he had a considerable potbelly. His expression was bored. "Yes?" he asked in a tone clearly indicating he didn't relish the interruption.

"I'm Dr. Cartier, Captain," Yak said. "I have two patients to be transferred from the plane outside to an ambulance that will be here momentarily. May I borrow three of your guards to help make the transfer? Oh, you've probably been informed already that I'll be flying out of here with four different patients when I return." He smiled. "It is the general's release of the Norte Americano hostages to celebrate the holiday."

"I seem to remember hearing something about it last night," Gonzalez lied. "You have the necessary papers?"

Yak tightened up his smile as if in disapproval of the query. "Captain," he said reproachfully, "this is the general's personal order."

Gonzalez shrugged. He walked to the wall at the end of the office and kicked it vigorously. "Sergeant!" he boomed. When a shaggy head appeared in the office doorway in answer to the summons, the potbellied little captain pointed to Yak and Rafael. "Take two men and go with them to move two patients into an ambulance."

The sergeant, a weatherbeaten, rangy-looking man, saluted slackly. He disappeared for an instant, then returned with two young soldiers. The trio led the way along the corridor to the tarmac outside. Rafael fell into step beside Yak. "Imagine bein' lucky enough to bag a sergeant's uniform!" he gloated in a whisper.

Yak couldn't restrain a smile. It was so like Rafael's natural ebullience to consider the sergeant's uniform as already acquired while the sergeant himself still remained to be dealt with. The man would have stopped at Sweetie-Pie's Beechcraft ambulance plane, but Yak waved him on to the Nord. The sergeant looked confused, but he continued on.

The Nord's cabin door was open again and the step platform was in place. No one was visible inside. Rafael elbowed the privates aside so that he followed directly behind the sergeant while the man mounted the steps. At the top, with his bulk shielding the movement from the soldiers below, Rafael swung the butt of the carbine hard against the sergeant's head. The bludgeoned man pitched forward without making a sound, and Gary and David caught him in midslump and dragged him to one side. Rafael stepped inside and moved in the other direction, leaving the cabin doorway clear.

The second man was watching where he put his feet down upon the platform steps. When he looked up, KO's hands were already closing upon his throat. The soldier vanished inside without even a squeak of sound, but the third man had been looking directly at his predecessor and had witnessed the vanishing act. He stopped dead.

Yak, right behind him, prodded the man in the back with the Smith & Wesson Model 59 that KO had given him at the airstrip. "Inside," Yak said tersely. "Quietly."

Reluctantly, the man moved forward. Inside, he was at once engulfed in David McCarter's ferocious bear hug. In seconds he was unconscious. McCarter pitched the body to one side where it landed on top of the others.

Yak had started to close the cabin door, but paused. "Get with it changing into those uniforms," he said. "Here's Sweetie-Pie with the ambulance."

He went outside and down the steps to join the Frenchman who was standing beside a white, boxy-looking vehicle, talking to the driver.

Behind him, Yak heard the cabin door close again.

30

Gary was the first one dressed in the newly conscripted uniform. He dodged out of the melee of bodies thrashing about in the confined space as the others tried on and discarded parts of uniforms. Rafael had confiscated the sergeant's shirt. Muttered curses in three languages filled the air as the trio kept bumping into each other. KO and David were blessed—or cursed—with the same upper-body bulk that made attempting to get into the uniforms such a frustrating experience, but they were managing.

Gary worked his way down the aisle past the broken-out slats from the empty crates. He stepped into the cockpit where Ian Revill was resting in the copilot's seat, slumped against the headrest. He was bound into the seat at shoulders and ankles so that if for any reason the Phoenix Force group didn't return to the airport Revill could claim he had been coerced into the whole bizarre affair. Revill turned his head to look at Gary in his ill-fitting uniform, and a ghost of a smile trembled at the corners of his drawn-looking mouth.

"We're leaving now," Gary told him. "We won't be long."

"Do it right," Revill said.

"Bet on it," Gary said. For a fleeting instant he

wondered at the bravado that seemed to be welling up inside him. He had never felt so alive. He dropped a hand lightly on Revill's shoulder. "Sweetie-Pie will taxi you to the pumps and gas the plane up."

Revill nodded to show that he understood. "Bon voyage," he said.

Gary squeezed the shoulder under his hand lightly, left the cockpit, and traversed the aisle again. The others had shaken themselves down into some sort of order, and they looked at him expectantly. Gary threw open the cabin door and descended the platform steps to the macadam. Yak stood at the opened doors at the rear of the ambulance, pulling out a canvas stretcher. Sweetie-Pie was still talking to the driver.

The one variable in Yak's detailed plan had concerned the size of the ambulance. Any size would transport the five of them to The Holding Place, but unless the ambulance was large, they would require a second vehicle to get themselves and four hostages back to the airport.

This ambulance was small.

Gary joined Yak at the rear of the vehicle and peered inside. One look was enough. "This thing looks more like a morgue wagon than an ambulance," he grumbled. The amenities consisted of two more stretchers whose handles fitted into slots. There were two leather pads, less than body length, running along the sides. The "ambulance" was a delivery van, and an ancient one at that.

Yak handed a stretcher to Gary who carried it back into the plane. David met him at the rear and they bundled the bound and gagged guerilla into it. "He shouldn't want to call any attention to himself,'' David had said of the gag, ''but let's play it safe.'' They carried the man out to the ambulance and dumped him onto one of the leather pads.

They carried the stretcher inside again, spread it in the aisle, and Rafael placed himself upon it. Gary picked up an Uzi and tucked it beneath Rafael's thigh so it was concealed. He added a pouch of the extra clips he had loaded with the Uzi's 9mm ammunition. Then he and David picked up the stretcher handles again and carried Rafael out. They slid the stretcher aboard where Rafael remained upon it, weapon hidden.

They did the same with KO after Gary had once again put an Uzi and a pouch of clips beneath KO's leg. No one at the freight depot seemed to be paying any attention to the activities going on at the planes and the ambulance. Why should they? They had presented themselves at the guard commandment's office and everything was being done under his auspices, wasn't it?

They returned again to the plane, where David picked up a white cloth sack of reddish brown berries that Rafael had harvested at the river airstrip before their departure. David crushed the bottom of the sack between his powerful hands and a brown liquid oozed slowly from the sack's pores. David and Gary rubbed it on their hands and faces, transforming their visible coloration into that of Rafael and KO, and more importantly, into that of a majority of the members of the Paraguayan Army.

David picked up his own shirt and tossed it carelessly over the shoulder of his uniform shirt. Beneath it he concealed the third Uzi. Gary slipped into the straps of the backpack containing the hand grenades, and they moved out onto the top step of the platform. They waited there until Sweetie-Pie, breaking off his casual conversation with the ambulance driver, sauntered over to them.

The Frenchman ascended the steps, went past them, and entered the cabin. Gary waited until he heard the thud of the locking bolt being thrown over before he followed David down to the rear of the ambulance. The plan called for Sweetie-Pie to taxi the Nord to the service area and gas it up, then give it slow service until he saw the ambulance return. If it didn't, he would go back to his own previously serviced Beechcraft and fly back to his home base.

"The driver?" David had just asked Yak when Gary arrived.

"Not here," Yak returned. "He might be known at the exit gate." He was pulling on a white smock he had found in the van. "Ride with him. When you reach a quiet area, pull him over and put his lights out. Then you drive."

McCarter nodded. Back in England he was a successful rally driver. "Ready," Gary said to Yak in response to an inquiring look after David departed for the front of the ambulance. He and Yak climbed in and closed and latched the rear doors. The ambulance pulled away, and they all remained silent, each with his hand upon a weapon, while it crossed the tarmac, slowed for the exit gate, and then in response to a genial shout from the guard post, speeded up again.

Gary found himself grinning foolishly. Yak sat

with his back to the closed rear doors lighting up an American cigarette he produced from somewhere in his clothing. Rafael and KO, the time for playacting over, shoved their stretchers aside and sat cross-legged with their Uzis balanced across their thighs.

Then the ambulance slowed, pulled to the right, and stopped. "Ahh!" Yak said softly. He looked regretful as he crushed out his cigarette. He faced about and unlatched the rear doors. The Uzis were underneath the stretchers. David McCarter jerked the curb-side door open. He still had his shirt dangling over his shoulder, and there was still a bulge beneath it.

"This looked like a good place to dump him," David said. "A slum. Nobody around. Who wants to give me a hand?"

Gary slithered across a leather pad and stepped down onto the street, which was cobblestoned with a light layering of asphalt on top. It was a short street with small shacks on either side sitting crookedly on low stilts. Gary followed McCarter around to the front of the ambulance where David opened the driver's-side door.

Gary caught one quick glimpse of the driver slumped over the steering wheel before McCarter jerked him out from under it onto the street. Gary captured a flopping arm. Together they carried the man to a low fence with more pickets missing than present and dropped him behind it. *"Borracho!"* David said loudly. He plucked the hat from the lolling head and pulled it down over the face.

KO was standing at the rear of the ambulance when they recrossed the street. He had a thoughtful look on his face. He was looking along a muddy cross alley a few feet behind where they had stopped. He gestured toward the alley when David and Gary came up to him.

The alley was perhaps fifty feet long.

At its far end, parked on the far side of the next parallel street, sat an empty, dark green, military Jeep.

31

"I vote yes!" David McCarter exclaimed immediately.

Rafael's head popped out of the back of the ambulance. "What are we voting on?" he demanded. Yak's head appeared beside Rafael's.

KO pointed toward the Jeep. Rafael's face lit up, but then he shook his head. "It must have stranded itself," he warned.

"It's worth a look!" David declared energetically. "Come on!"

He led the way into the alley. KO followed, then Gary. "You stay with bozo," Rafael said to Yak, jerking a thumb toward the guerilla's mummified figure. Yak leaned against the rear of the ambulance. Rafael took an uneasy look around the street. "This place is too damn *quiet*!" he complained. A young boy came out of a shack across the street, and Rafael called to him. "Hey, where *is* everybody?"

"At the parade," the boy said. "We're going to be late. My father is still getting ready."

"Yeah, sure, the national holiday," Rafael muttered after waving to the youngster. Yak had unhurriedly closed the ambulance doors when the young boy appeared. "You think this is a good idea?" Rafael asked, gesturing toward the alley.

"We need that one, or another one," Yak said. "Let KO see what he can do."

"Okay," Rafael said and trotted up the alley after the others, splashing accumulated rainwater with every stride. KO had the hood of the Jeep raised and had pulled up the sleeve of his acquired uniform to disclose wire wound around his upper forearm. He worked it loose and held in his hand two individual wires with bulldog clips at their ends. His dark head disappeared into the engine compartment.

"Get in and give it some gas," he said to David. When McCarter complied, the engine started with a roar. KO stripped off his hot-wiring apparatus and slammed the hood down.

"Someone must have stopped for a noon nap before the parade," Rafael said above the engine sound. "Let's move."

David slid over to let Rafael take the wheel. KO and Gary jumped into the back. Rafael cut a tight semicircle and wheeled the Jeep through the alley, shooting mud up on the walls on both sides. He pulled the Jeep up behind the ambulance. David hurried immediately to the ambulance's driver's seat.

"Beautiful," Yak said. "KO, stay with Rafael. Gary, inside with me." He latched the rear doors again when they were in.

David had them moving again almost immediately. Rafael followed two car lengths behind. "Sure as hell makes us look official," he said to KO who had climbed over the back of the front seat to sit beside him. "I can't picture anyone pulling us over to take a look at us now."

They had a five-mile run in silence then, the later

stages of which showed increasing signs of civilization. They burst from a suburb into the city proper
almost without warning. They crossed a main street,
the curb of which was lined with sawhorses. "Parade
route," Rafael said almost to himself. "Only two
more blocks now."

The ambulance turned left and Rafael followed.
When David pulled in to the curb, Rafael was right
behind him, leaving just enough room to open the
ambulance's rear doors. KO and Gary jumped out
while Rafael examined the street, trying to pick out
the building they wanted. Ian Revill had told them
The Holding Place had no street number.

KO opened the ambulance doors. Yak pushed the
tied-up guerilla out to the edge of the van. KO and
Gary stood him up on his feet. Almost at once the
man began to make burbling noises behind his gag.
His bulging eyes were fixed upon a nondescript one-
story building across the street different from its
neighbors only in that it had a black door.

"He knows," Gary said softly to KO. "He
knows."

Rafael had caught the guerilla's reaction, too.
They started across the street, Gary and KO muscling
the guerilla between them. Yak smoothed out the
wrinkles in his white smock and straightened his
beret. Rafael and KO carried their Uzis openly. Mc-
Carter's was still under the loose folds of his shirt.

The black door was locked. Rafael pounded upon
it, then saw a button in the upper left hand corner.
He pressed it and seconds later there was a loud buzz.
Rafael pushed against the door, which opened. He
stepped inside cautiously, holding the others back

with his palm outstretched behind him until he saw he was in a boxlike place at the top of a flight of stairs with no one in sight.

"What the hell do you want?" a voice shouted.

Rafael looked downward in the direction of the voice. A flight of wooden steps stretched straight down, broken up only by three intermediate landings marking the three floors below street level. Rafael stepped forward to the top of the stairs and raised his own voice. "Sergeant Caceres bringing in another of that group from yesterday for your workshop," he shouted back.

The man at the foot of the stairs was in civilian attire. He was tall and thin and wore a black patch over his left eye. "Bring him down," the man said, then disappeared.

Rafael started down the stairs slowly, the butt of the Uzi in his armpit. The treads of the steps were worn in the center by the passage of many unhappy feet. The first landing had an open door to the right, which disclosed a long line of empty cells. The second landing disclosed the same thing except the cells were occupied.

Behind him Rafael could hear the scraping sounds as KO and Gary carried the writhing guerilla down the stairs. "Kind of casual, aren't they?" David McCarter's mutter reached Rafael's ears.

"Who comes here willingly?" Rafael asked with a shrug.

He stepped down from the last of the stairs onto a dirty cement floor. The same type of door as at the landings was on his right, and he moved through it briskly, his Uzi unobtrusive-looking but ready. The black-eyepatched man was behind a counter. In an instant Rafael took in not only the six open-barred cells to the right, but the door in the room's white-washed wall to the left. Another black door. Rafael's nostrils absorbed the unpleasant odor of sweat, blood, pain and fear. The entire floor area was littered with old newspapers, filthy coffee containers and discarded cigarette packs.

The eyepatched man was looking at the guerilla. "Throw him in one of the cells," he said. "I'm short-handed this morning. They took most of my people and put them into uniforms to beef up the parade."

Rafael motioned toward the cells, and KO and Gary carried the guerilla to the nearest one. "Lots of machinery you people are carrying," the man commented to Rafael. "Oh, sure, that's for the parade, too, right?" His attention had shifted to Yak in his white smock.

"This is Dr. Cartier," Rafael said. "He's here to oversee the transfer of the hostages who were brought in here yesterday."

"You've got a paper says that?" the man asked.

Rafael smiled. "No paper." He paused as somewhere behind the black door he heard a man scream.

"That's Luis," the black-eyepatched man said with a laugh that was almost a giggle. "He works even on holidays."

"No papers," Rafael said again. "But call Captain Gonzalez, the guard commandant at the airport freight depot. He'll tell you it's the general's orders the hostages are to be flown out today."

"Gonzalez, eh?" The tall man turned to the telephone on the desk behind him. He spoke into it for several minutes in a low tone while Rafael waited tensely. When he turned around, he was laughing. "Gonzalez is mad at you for walking off with his men on a day he's shorthanded, too," he said. "I can't leave the phone. Here." He tossed a bunch of keys across the counter to Rafael. "Get them out yourself. They're in the first four cells on the left on the second floor."

Rafael deflected the keys while they were still in the air, and Gary caught them deftly. "Put them in the ambulance," Rafael said. "Go with him, KO. You, too, Doctor." Gary and KO turned immediately and started to leave the room. When they were going through the doorway, Rafael spoke again, in pig latin. "Utca etha elephoneta inela." He grinned at the eyepatched man. "That's how I tell them double-goddamn quick."

Yak had hesitated, but he followed Gary and KO. David lounged against a wall, his loosely draped shirt still concealing his Uzi. Rafael's was dangling in his left hand. Two minutes passed. "Where are you taking them?" the tall man asked. He was leaning on his elbows on the counter. "I'm surprised the general isn't here himself with the photographers."

"The general *here*?" Rafael asked scornfully.

The eyepatched man laughed. "Well, perhaps not. We—"

He broke off as the black door at the far end of the room opened. A stocky, bald man strode into the room. He was wearing a flowered sportshirt and cream colored slacks. Behind him two men were supporting a naked man who was bleeding on them. He looked like a native farmer. His entire body was twitching uncontrollably, and he was babbling loudly in Spanish. A fourth man walked behind him.

The bald man walked toward the desk. "He's ready to talk to you now, Pirovano," he said. He turned to look at Rafael, then did a double take at the sight of the Uzi. "Where the hell did you get that?" he demanded.

"This is Sergeant Caceres, Luis," Pirovano explained. "He has come to transfer the hostages."

"Transfer—?" Luis wheeled toward the desk. "Don't you ever check anything out, man? That's not Caceres!" He flicked a glance at David. "And neither is that one! What's going on here?"

He was advancing rapidly upon Rafael as he spoke, and he tried to kick the Uzi out of Rafael's hand. The second he was within reach, Rafael hit him with a solid, right-hand smash to the mouth. The first part of Luis to hit the cement floor was the back of his head and he slid when he landed.

Behind Rafael, David's Uzi fired a four-shot warning burst as the men supporting the naked man dropped him and reached for weapons. They then forgot the weapons and dropped to the floor, using the man's body as a buffer.

Rafael felt a sharp pain in his right hand. Broken finger, he thought, but when he looked he saw a piece of tooth imbedded in the middle knuckle. He brushed it away impatiently. Behind the counter, Pirovano made a lunge for the top drawer of his desk. Rafael pivoted, clamped his Uzi to his hip, and fired a burst that walked across the back of Pirovano's neck. He crashed through his desk which collapsed around him with a shriek of dismantled wood.

Two more men burst into the room from behind the open black door. David's and Rafael's crossing fire sent stone chips into their faces as they ducked back inside. David lined up on the tangle of men on the floor who were now grabbing at their weapons. He emptied his clip with a prolonged, hammering fusillade that sent a stream of bullets through the naked victim's body into those of the men trying to use him as a shield.

"Time to go," Rafael said grimly.

They backed through the doorway together.

There was no movement in the room they had left, but both men knew there would be a lot of movement soon.

32

Rafael and David backed slowly up the stairs to the first landing, then waited. David separated the L-clip of his Uzi and inserted a fresh magazine. A carbine was poked through the doorway below them, and they both fired at it simultaneously. The carbine was hastily withdrawn, and the doorway remained clear.

"Come up another flight," Gary's voice called down to them. He was kneeling on the second landing, and he had hand grenades and satchel charges spread out beside him. "Come on, guys," he insisted. "Yak and KO are taking the last hostage, Muriel, to the street."

David and Rafael moved backward to Gary's landing, eyes still fixed upon the doorway below. Nobody showed. Rafael looked down at Gary's array of weapons. "What the hell is this?"

"Watch," Gary said confidently.

He picked up a grenade, pulled the pin and threw the grenade against the stairway wall. From there it angled to the bottom wall, from which it dropped and rolled through the doorway. There were yells of alarm followed by a muffled, "Crump!" The yells turned to screams of pain.

"What a billiard shot!" David said admiringly.

"Evidence of a misspent youth," Gary informed him. "Let's get up to the next landing."

He and David stuffed pineapples in their pockets. Gary picked up three of the satchel charges. David carried the backpack. Rafael kept his Uzi lined up on the empty doorway as all three backed up to the next landing.

The satchel charges were a number of blocks of explosives attached to a board which was then covered in tannish brown canvas. They measured a foot square by two inches thick and weighed fifteen pounds. Gary touched off the fuse on one and sent it clattering down the steps with a bowling ball-like swing of his arm.

The foot-square, canvas-covered lethal weapon erupted in the middle of the lowest flight of steps. The stairs jumped up into the air and disintegrated in a shower of splinters. When they could see clearly again, the second landing was still there with the second flight of stairs canting drunkenly from it, but below that was nothing. They had all felt the tremor which had shaken the top landing upon which they were standing.

"One more time," Gary said. He motioned for the others to back off the landing onto the concrete of the box-like space inside the outer door. He tossed another satchel charge down the steps. When it exploded, there was still a top landing but no stairs at all.

"I could have dumped the two floors of cell blocks down on their asses if it wasn't for the prisoners," Gary said calmly.

"I'd say it was hardly necessary," McCarter returned.

"Yeah," Rafael agreed. "And I'd say no one's

coming after us from this direction till they build some new stairs."

"There's got to be a rear exit," David argued. "But maybe not, with the kind of snakepit they're operating down there."

"Whatever, let's put it in gear and ramble," Rafael said. He opened the outside door, then hurriedly closed it all but a crack when a blast of martial music hit them. "What the hell? Ahh, the parade!" he told himself. He had not seen Yak running across the street, and he opened the door to admit him. "Is the phone line cut?" he asked before Yak could speak.

"KO is unhappy because he chipped his knife blade cutting it."

"If there's no rear exit, we've cut this caper," Rafael said.

"The parade is a problem," Yak said. "It's moving along the avenue we have to cross to get back to the airport."

"No perspiration," David declared. "Rafael, you take the ambulance." He grinned at them. "What tickles me, fellas, is I turned out to be the sort of guy my parents warned me against." He headed for the Jeep.

Gary caught up to him in the middle of the street. "Cover that thing up!" he blurted, looking at the Uzi in McCarter's hand.

"The crowd today must already have seen more weapons than they knew existed," David said. "What's a few more?"

He settled himself under the steering wheel with Gary beside him. The engines of both vehicles had been left running. David made a big circling move-

ment with his arm to let Rafael, driving the ambulance, know that he was going to make a one-
hundred-and-eighty-degree turn and go back the way
they had come. What they didn't need now was to get
themselves lost or dead-ended on side streets.

"Rafael's right behind me?" he asked Gary as the
Jeep approached the main avenue. He was intent
upon his driving.

"Right behind."

"Good." David edged into the intersection, then
sliced between two marching units and stopped. The
oncoming platoon came up to the Jeep and the flanks
rippled around it. Marching men piled up behind
standing men. The platoon's ranks bulged and then
burst. Men spilled out across both sidewalks.

A murmur in the ranks swelled to an angry growl.
David stood up on the seat of the Jeep with his Uzi
held across his chest. He bellowed something unintelligible while he circled his right arm widely again to
indicate to Rafael that the ambulance should take advantage of the gap in the parade the Jeep had
created.

The sight of his intimidating figure served its purpose. Quick-witted noncoms to the rear of the melee
halted their men and prevented further piling up of
the troops. When the ambulance rolled through the
intersection, David sat down again and followed with
the Jeep. A few voices were still raised in shouts, but
the majority of the marchers now didn't seem to find
it unreasonable that an ambulance should have the
right of way.

"More brass than a foundry!" Gary muttered
enviously.

The two-vehicle parade encountered no more problems.

"Relief driver," Rafael said to the guard at the airport freight depot entrance.

"Hey, Captain Gonzalez wants to see you guys right away!" the guard informed him.

"Right away," Rafael assured him solemnly.

Rafael drove out to the Nord. Once again David pulled the Jeep in right behind the ambulance. Sweetie-Pie had been watching for them. The cabin door of the Nord opened and the little Frenchman descended the platform steps to the tarmac. He had both hands clasped above his head, shaking them vigorously in the manner of a winning prizefighter. He then walked the hundred yards to his Beechcraft.

He was already taxiing out to the end of the runway for takeoff while the Phoenix five were still transferring the four hostages from the ambulance to the Nord.

The Beechcraft was in the air when David McCarter sat down in the pilot's seat of the Nord and began running through its preflight checklist with Ian Revill.

Nine minutes later Revill turned on the radio to ask the tower in his clipped, assured British accent for takeoff clearance.

Eighteen minutes after Rafael had driven through the airport gate, the Nord was also in the air.

33

Yak, Rafael, Gary and KO sat limply for the first hour of flight, occasionally glancing at each other. Conversation was desultory. They were recharging batteries almost totally expended. With the plane in the air and David's course charted for him, Rafael and KO had removed Ian Revill from the copilot's seat and made him as comfortable as possible in the cabin, stretched across two seats with the middle arm removed.

Rafael was the first to rouse himself. "Housekeepin' time," he announced, standing up. He went to the rear of the plane and dragged a guard's body to the cabin door. Gary and KO followed suit. Rafael waved Yak off and towed the fourth body down the aisle.

It took Rafael and KO both to open the cabin door against the pressure. KO wedged it. "Okay, flyin' lesson time for these types," Rafael said. He pushed the first body out the door. One by one the others followed. Rafael had cannily seated the hostages at the front of the plane where his housekeeping tactics couldn't be seen by them.

The weapons went next, all that hadn't been used plus those that had. "Sweetie-Pie would have a fit if he could see this," Gary said while pitching out the remainder of his grenades.

Last out were the broken-up crates in which the

weapons had been packed. A five-minute spruce-up job followed, and they were ready for whatever inspection awaited them in Rio de Janeiro. KO unblocked the cabin door and he and Rafael closed it.

KO handed Yak a penciled note. "Mr. Fusaka's address," KO said.

Yak smiled. "We'll take care of him," he promised. "Handsomely." He knelt down in the aisle alongside Ian Revill's two-seat bed. "How's it going?" he asked.

"Tolerably," Revill said.

"As soon as we reach Rio, we'll move you and the hostages to Star of the Sea Hospital there." He glanced toward the front of the plane. "I think they are just short of outright shock status."

"Have you talked to them to find out which was your prime target for rescue?"

"Not yet."

"I have an opinion on it, of course, but I'm going to let someone else ask the questions," Yak said. "Those four people are but one degree removed from cracking up like dropped eggs. They've had enough for now, and still have to go through debriefing in Washington. But we've got our person out alive. Not too healthy, but breathing. And we, all five, are also still breathing. The mission is over. We've played the game, done the job, and delivered the package—*Gott zei dank*, as they say back home."

Rafael wandered up into the cockpit where he appropriated the copilot's seat. David looked over and gave him a thumbs-up sign. Rafael smiled, but quickly turned serious.

"Back there in that sinkhole...with that poor

farmer they were torturing, and used as a shield—"
he began.

"I did the guy a favor," David said.

"If you say so. I could have done it," Rafael continued, "but I was just as glad you decided it was
necessary before I did. I mean—"

"It was bloody well necessary," David rasped,
"like all this shit we plow through. For every ounce
of gain or glory we have to buy a gallon of gore. As
long as it isn't ours, I guess we're doing it right.
Right?"

"Meanwhile, back at the farm," Rafael joked, "I
wonder what our friends know about all this. Whoever takes down this report is going to have one
helluva script."

"Yeah," David said. "And I can hardly wait for
the next one."

The Nord flew on through the dying sunlight.

PHOENIX FORCE

#1 Argentine Deadline

ON SALE NOW!

Phoenix Force is a five-man army of such dedication that its toughness is challenged to the limits of endurance every month of the year. It is always a foul assignment for Phoenix Force, in whatever jungle or desert they find themselves—fully armed but forever on their own.

ARGENTINE DEADLINE tells the exciting story of a group of U.S. citizens who are abducted, then threatened within an inch of their lives. Indeed, the threat is to cut off the head of one captive for every day a huge ransom remains unpaid. Phoenix Force is fighting against time. The task calls for fearless courage and ingenuity from each man in the outfit. Here is a scene involving the rugged Canadian, Gary Manning:

"All right," said Gary. "Let's get started."

A line of eucalyptus trees appeared, marking the presence of a ranch. Police sergeant Rojas eased off the gas, and the Fiat rolled to a stop just before they reached the lane that led to the *estancia*.

From the trunk, Rojas produced a pair of PA 3-DM submachine guns (Uzi-type) and for Gary an M1907 Mannlicher pistol. Manning stripped out of his jacket and belted on the pistol, then checked the position of the Gerber Mark 1 sheath knife to make sure he could reach it easily over his shoulder.

The sun fell through the eucalyptus, dappling the lane and making Gary blink as shadow and light alternated across his face. The temperature was a measure cooler under the trees and the air was blessedly free of dust.

The lane was half a kilometer long, the trees stopping as though cut with a machete as the road opened into the yard of the *estancia*. In front of the house, one of the military trucks sat disabled. Two fatigue-clad men were working beneath its hood.

Gary moved back into the shade, motioning for Rojas to do the same. The house was another half-kilometer on, but the way was completely open. Only a wheat field divided the end of the lane and the men at the truck.

"I'm going to cut through the wheat," said Gary.

Rojas nodded. "Very well. I will stay here unless you signal me to come in."

Gary clapped him on the shoulder and crouched low, not seeing the tightening of Rojas's eyes behind the sunglasses. He cut into the wheat and moved through the field quickly, real low, the sun beating down heavily on his back. He stopped twice to get his bearings.

The men working on the truck were gone. The

house brooded silently behind blank windows. For the first time he realized there were no power lines going in, no telephone cable. He looked toward the lane but saw no sign of Rojas.

Sweat trickled into the corner of one eye. It was still only midmorning and the sun was brutal. No telling how long it would take for the reinforcements to arrive. He could dehydrate, waiting for them.

Checking the safeties of his weapon, he worked the action—and broke from the wheat.

In three strides Gary was running flat out while keeping a low profile. At his present rate of speed, he would reach shelter in less than nine seconds. . . .

Gunfire exploded from the house, the slugs tearing a line of dust behind Gary's heels. He leaped forward and dived, rolling over and over until he could bring the weapon on the source of the fire. He pressed the trigger. . . .

Nothing happened.

Cursing, Gary rolled again as the hidden gunman released another burst that came close enough to sting as the slugs tore pebbles apart. He got to his feet and ran toward shelter again, making a desperate dive for cover.

Sucking in short breaths, Gary checked the action of the PA 3-DM and once more pulled the trigger with the same result: the gun would not fire. He threw it aside in anger and drew the pistol; he checked that. It also would not fire.

There was no question left in his mind. Rojas had bollixed both weapons. The policeman had gone over to the terrorists. That was why there was no covering fire from the lane.

And most likely no reinforcements on the way.

During the moment of action, Gary had cursed aloud. But now he wasted no more breath, no thoughts on recriminations. What was done was done. The past could not be changed. And the people in the house assumed that he was without weapons, done in by Rojas's treachery.

In a moment someone would be coming after him. That would be their second mistake.

ABLE TEAM

PHOENIX FORCE

These new series have been produced by Don Pendleton in the bestselling tradition of THE EXECUTIONER. Like Mack Bolan, the men of Able Team and Phoenix Force are fighters for ultimate justice, even when it has to be above and beyond the law.

Don Pendleton would like to hear from you about these books. He invites you to write to him to give your views on Mack's new avenger teams. Your response will ensure exciting new directions for Able Team and Phoenix Force, with damn fine stories to keep you reading. Write to:

Don Pendleton
c/o Gold Eagle Books
P.O. Box 22188
Tempe, AZ 85281